MOONLIGHT EXCEPTION

Agents of HIS Novel

SHEILA KELL

Moonlight Exception
Copyright @ 2025 by Sheila Kell
Cunningham Publishing

Editing and Formatting: Lea Schizas
Photographer: Paul Henry Serres Photography
Model: Simon Chev

ISBN (Print): 978-1-957587-17-2
ISBN (EBook): 978-1-957587-16-5

Printed in the USA

DEDICATION

To Samantha Necaise, aka Summer N. Dawn. Thank you for writing sprints with me every morning to get the creative juices flowing. I never would have met my deadline without you!

Titles by Sheila Kell

HIS Series
His Desire
His Choice
His Return
His Chance
His Destiny
His Family
His Heart
His Fantasy
A Hamilton Christmas

Agents of HIS Series
Evening Shadows
Midnight Escape
Afternoon Delight
Bayou Sunset
Chasing Shadows at Dusk
Moonlight Exception

Coastal Investigation Series
Deadly Betrayal
Read Between the Lines
Fractured Trust

Chapter One

RODNEY "DOC" WHITE barely had time to react before a shadowy figure lunged at him, brandishing a large knife. In an instant, the blade sliced through the air and grazed the skin of Doc's arm, leaving a sharp sting and catching him completely off guard.

His heart pounded, a wild drumbeat of adrenaline, but then an unexpected wave of tranquility washed over him, a familiar sensation that often came during unanticipated confrontations. Even in the gritty streets of Baltimore, Maryland, with a young kid standing before him—half his age and size—he felt a strange sense of composure settle in as if he were floating above the moment's chaos. The city buzzed with life around them, but everything else faded into the background instantly. Ready for the fight, Doc fixed his determined gaze on his assailant, studying the punk's every twitch and micro-expression as he anticipated the next move in their standoff.

"You don't want to do this, kid," Doc warned, his raspy voice laced with concern and authority. He stood near the entrance of the dimly lit alley, shadows flickering around him as he watched the youth. The young man's posture conveyed uncertainty, yet he carried himself with a bravado that revealed his nervousness. The whispers of a gang initiation hung in the air, and the stakes were perilously high.

Doc's muscular build resembled a linebacker's—strong and imposing, but lacking the bulk typically associated with such a physique. This made him a target, a prize the gang members set their sights on. They believed taking him down would showcase their strength and elevate their status.

"You have no idea what I'm capable of, old man," the kid spat, his voice dripping with defiance as he tried to maneuver in a tight circle around Doc. The knife's blade gleamed menacingly under the harsh glow of the streetlight, reflecting light with a flickering brightness as he waved it back and forth with reckless energy.

In his peripheral vision, Doc noticed his long-time friend Simon engaged in a tense standoff with another kid, who held a large knife ominously. The four faced off, their eyes locked in a battle of wills, creating a scene charged with palpable tension. Amid the chaos, Doc's initial thought was a curious relief that at least the kids were only armed with knives, keeping the confrontation from escalating into something even more dangerous.

"Simon," Doc called out, his voice laced with concern, "are you ready for this?" Doc's apprehension seeped through despite his attempts to hide it. Simon stood beside him, a stark contrast to Doc's battle-worn demeanor. As a firefighter in Kissimmee, Florida, Simon had always been the steady hand amidst chaos, but he wasn't used to the relentless struggle for survival that Doc faced so often.

"Enough talk, old man," the kid across from Doc said before lunging, the telltale glint of the knife arcing high above his head.

Doc braced himself, instinctively raising his forearm to intercept the incoming strike, grateful it was his uninjured arm. With precise timing, he countered with a powerful punch that struck the kid's stomach, forcing the young fighter to double over, gasping for breath. The impact echoed through the air, a testament to Doc's skill and determination in the heat of the moment.

As a former SEAL, Doc had a keen instinct for understanding the ebb and flow of combat. He could quickly gauge when to hold back his formidable strength and when to unleash the full force of his considerable size. Standing at six feet four inches with a muscular build honed by years of rigorous training, Doc understood that this young fighter, despite his bravado, was unprepared to withstand the raw power that his massive frame could deliver.

Doc hesitated. His instincts urged him to scare the kid off and foster a sense of caution, but not so far as to send him to the hospital. The last thing he wanted was to turn a moment of folly into a serious incident for the reckless little fool.

"How are you holding up, Simon?" Doc asked, watching the young man standing in front of him. The boy fixed his dark eyes on Doc with an intensity that could cut through steel.

"Is this what counts as a welcoming party in Baltimore?" Simon replied, a hint of amusement tinging his voice despite the tension in the air. "Because it definitely leaves much to be desired in terms of hospitality."

Although they came from the same hometown, Doc and Simon's paths didn't cross until college, where both pursued pre-med degrees. However, fate took an unexpected turn, leading them to become paramedics instead.

After the tragic loss of his older brother, a distinguished Navy SEAL who had bravely fought and died in combat, Doc felt a profound sense of duty and resolve ignite within him. Driven to honor his brother's legacy and protect his fellow countrymen and women, he enlisted in the Navy. With each grueling training session and challenge, Doc was determined to serve his country with the same courage and dedication his brother had shown.

"Son of a bitch!" Simon shouted, his voice tinged with pain. Whether his wound was a minor scrape or something more serious, Doc couldn't take his eyes off the enemy in front of them to properly evaluate Simon's injury.

"You okay?" Doc asked, his tone urgent yet steady, understanding that the playful banter had to stop. Adrenaline surged through him, driving him to take charge of the situation and bring the chaotic fight to a quick conclusion.

As silence lingered in the air and Simon's lack of response weighed heavily on his mind, Doc made a critical error—he turned his head to glance at his friend, a moment of distraction that could have dire consequences. The young man lunged forward with an unexpected burst of energy, catching Doc off guard again. This time, however, the blade did not find its mark on his forearm. Instead, the air crackled with tension as Doc instinctively shifted, narrowly avoiding the sharp edge.

Raw anger surged through Doc at the sight of his friend lying in the cobblestone alleyway, dark blood pooling beneath him. He squared his shoulders and planted his feet firmly on the ground, his eyes locked onto his attacker, determined to take him down. But in the heat of the moment, Doc felt a chill run down his spine as he realized that the second assailant had slipped out of view, a shadow lurking somewhere nearby.

At that moment, a sudden, intense pain shot through him as the cold steel of a knife pierced deep into his back, leaving him momentarily breathless with shock.

"Run, Chuck!" one kid shouted as they dashed away.

Doc fell to his knees, the sharp crack echoing through the alleyway, a haunting sound that seemed to linger in the cool night air. Gritting his teeth against the pain, he reached behind him, his fingers trembling as they brushed over the warm, damp fabric of his jacket. There, he could feel the throbbing ache of the injury spreading like fire across his skin.

Doc crawled down the gritty alley, his hands and knees scraping against the rough pavement. Each inch felt like a battle against the stinging fear that twisted in his gut. He reached his friend, who lay unnaturally still. Doc barely registered the sounds outside the alleyway, yet the uncertainty of Simon's condition gripped his heart with icy fingers. Every instinct screamed at him, and guilt surged within him, a relentless tide. He couldn't shake the thought that he brought Simon to Baltimore and into this dark, foreboding alley in the Inner Harbor that had led them to this moment.

"Simon!" Doc shouted, desperation tinging his voice. His heart raced as he looked the battered figure before him. His hands trembled slightly as they grazed Simon's skin, searching for a pulse at the base of his neck. Anguish coursed through Doc, amplifying the searing pain that radiated up and down his spine, mingling with the warmth of blood trickling from his wound. The stark reality of the moment weighed heavily on him, fueling his fear as he assessed the severity of Simon's injuries.

Every second stretched into an eternity as he frantically searched for a pulse. Panic washed over him like ice water. Nothing. He couldn't bear the thought of losing Simon.

As the paramedic training surged to the forefront of his mind, he reached for his phone, his fingers trembling with urgency. Just as he was about to dial 911, the device slipped from his bloodied grasp, tumbling to the ground and cracking against the unforgiving cobblestone pavement. Time felt like it was slipping away as he realized he had only moments to act. Without hesitation, Doc painstakingly maneuvered his body over his friend, positioning himself to begin CPR, focusing on the task at hand, hoping to restore the spark of life with every compress and breath.

Desperate and breathless, he raised his voice, echoing through the dimly lit alleyway. "Help! Please, someone call 911!" His words bounced off the brick walls, blending with the distant sounds of the bustling city, hoping to reach anyone who could come to his aid.

"Oh, my God!" A panicked voice belonging to a striking blonde pierced the air as she dashed toward Doc, her eyes wide with urgency. "Laura, call 911! Stacy, take over CPR!"

"Julie, it's better not to get involved," another woman warned, her tone filled with concern as she turned to the frantic blonde. Doc felt a wave of frustration at her words.

"Nonsense, Laura!" the other woman retorted.

The beauty quickly kneeled beside him, her presence a fierce rallying point amid the chaos. "Hey, big guy! Move aside. We've got this!"

Doc's gaze locked onto Julie's, a silent plea evident on his face. "Save him," he implored, desperation lacing his voice.

In response, Julie appeared to understand the depth of his anxiety. Gently, she placed her arm around his shoulder, pulling him away from on top of his friend, her warmth providing comfort against the biting chill of the air.

"We'll do our best," she assured him, her voice steady—a beacon of hope amidst the chaos.

As Doc slowly slid away, worry continued to beat down on him. He turned back just in time to see Stacy spring into action, her hands skillfully performing CPR as she concentrated intently on the task. The sight filled him with a blend of fear and admiration. With a shaky breath escaping his lips, he settled onto the frigid cobblestones, the cold seeping through him as he watched, praying for a sliver of hope.

"You're bleeding!" Julie exclaimed, her voice filled with urgency. Her fingers gently probed the jagged wound on his back, sending a jolt of pain through him. He gritted his teeth, struggling against the sharp sting, but the physical agony faded compared to the overwhelming dread of losing his friend. Each breath he took felt heavy with the moment's weight, the world around them blurring into the background as he focused solely on Simon.

"I'm fine," he lied, his voice barely a whisper, unwilling to divert even a sliver of the vital attention from the frantic efforts to save his friend.

"You're not," Julie's calming voice cut through his focus, guiding his gaze like a beacon in the storm. When their eyes met—his deep blue mingling with her striking blue—he felt a peculiar sensation wash over him as if he were drifting away from reality.

But it wasn't the intoxicating rush of romance. Instead, it was the disorienting effects of his injury. With a determined shake of his head, Doc fought to dispel the fog creeping into his mind, straining against the encroaching darkness that threatened to consume the scene entirely. Each heartbeat echoed in his ears, amplifying the moment as he struggled to prevent his vision from narrowing into a painful tunnel.

"He's breathing," Stacy said, her voice steady but tinged with urgency as she placed her hand gently at the base of Simon's neck. "Tell them he's—"

Doc's gaze drifted away from Stacy's animated words to land squarely on Julie. With his heart pounding in his chest, he took a deep breath, his voice trembling slightly as he said, "Thank you." Then, without thinking, he opened his mouth and blurted out, "Will you marry me?" Just as the weight of his words filled the air, the world around him faded into darkness, and he felt the universe swirl away.

Chapter Two

AS THE SIRENS wailed in the night, Dr. Julie Banks and Stacy Mason, RN, alert and on call, quickly followed the ambulance in Julie's car. The glow of the flashing lights illuminated the road ahead. Upon arriving at the hospital, they exited the car and sprinted to the emergency room's ambulance entrance.

Tension filled the air inside the teaching hospital as Julie's clinical partner, Dr. Carlos Garcia, already in place, took charge of Simon's care, skillfully navigating the emergency room with calm determination. Meanwhile, Julie, focused and resolute, prepared to operate on Mr. White with her trauma nurse, Stacy, by her side, ready to assist and support her every move. The weight of the situation bore down on Julie as she readied herself to confront the challenge ahead.

"Don't dispose of the gloves we used at the scene," Julie reminded Stacy, her voice steady yet urgent as a nurse fastened a crisp, sterile apron around her. Although the atmosphere buzzed with an unspoken understanding, this was no ordinary situation. Julie, a trauma surgeon and part-time professor at the teaching hospital, had an obligation to explain to the students following her the reasons behind her actions. "Knowing the alleyway has been classified as a crime scene, it's important to preserve every piece of evidence—even the smallest detail can matter."

Julie shook her head, thinking of her friend Laura Wills, who had stood at the edge of the chaotic scene, clutching her phone to her ear as she relayed frantic details to the 911 operator. As she watched Julie and Stacy spring into action last night, she exclaimed, "Who carries disposable surgical gloves in their purse? That's just…strange."

"Did that include the clothes you put in the bag, Dr. Banks?" Darlene Lang asked, her brow furrowed with curiosity as she observed Julie and Stacy prepare. The second-year medical student had an inquisitive nature that often drove her to delve deeper into conversations. "I remember both of you carefully placing your clothes into separate bags and labeling them clearly. It makes me wonder—why would the police be interested in those items?"

"That's a great question, Miss Lang." Julie turned to Ryan Fair, a third-year medical student aiming to become a trauma surgeon. "And why is that, Mr. Fair?"

Ryan, ever prepared, stood tall and replied, "Because any evidence might have been transferred to your clothing or gloves while you assisted the victims, Dr. Banks."

"Correct." Julie glanced around the sterile, brightly lit room, her brow slightly furrowed with concern as she evaluated Stacy's preparedness. "All right," she said, her voice steady yet gentle, "if you're not ready for the surgery, you need to sit this one out or watch from the gallery."

The sounds of beeping monitors from the next room and the rustle of medical instruments filled the air, amplifying the moment's weight as she searched for her trailing students. She heard an "Aww" from Marla Rollins, a first-year, eager student who spent too much time preparing and missed most surgeries. Julie hadn't yet decided whether that was intentional. At that moment, she couldn't dwell on it. She had a patient who needed her attention.

With a swift motion, Julie nudged the adjoining door to the operating room open with her elbow, stepping into a whirlwind of activity. The sterile environment buzzed with the sounds of medical staff preparing for the upcoming surgery. Scrubs-clad nurses moved purposefully, their voices a soft murmur against the backdrop of beeping machines and rustling equipment. Julie's gaze fell on the anesthesiologist, who glanced back at her reassuringly, signaling that the patient was ready for the procedure.

"Okay, everyone," Julie said. "Let's see what we've got." She glanced up at the gallery and noticed several students yawning in attendance. She had no idea why they chose to watch her instead of Simon, but she would ensure they learned everything she could teach them without compromising her patient's health.

Rodney White was positioned on the surgical table, lying on his stomach, covered by a crisp white sheet from his hips down to ensure both modesty and warmth. With his head turned to the side, the anesthesiologist had easy access to his neck and face.

The room radiated a calm, focused atmosphere as the fluorescent lights illuminated the sterile environment.

After examining the X-rays on the lightboard mounted on the wall, Julie turned to Ryan and said, "What's your assessment, Mr. Fair?"

As the student cautiously approached, Julie's sharp eyes tracked his every movement while she monitored the patient's vital signs on the screen. Although the injured area was not life-threatening, it throbbed with an urgent need for attention, and Julie understood that any delay could complicate matters. She felt a weight of responsibility pressing on her, aware that time was critical to ensuring the patient's well-being.

Ryan cleared his throat from behind his mask. "Well, he has a laceration on his back that might indicate a hepatic injury. Without further evaluation, I can't determine if this is a serious liver injury, such as damage to the hepatic portal vein."

Julie raised an eyebrow at the assessment. "Miss Lang, can you tell if the hepatic portal vein has been damaged?"

Darlene nodded. "There isn't enough blood."

With a chuckle behind her mask, Julie said, "That's the gist of it, but later, you both will explain to me—in detail—ways to quickly assess the potential severity of an injury before you start the surgery. Believe me, you'll learn more when you open them up, but it's important to know what you're about to face."

The two students nodded. "Yes, Dr. Banks."

"Let's get started," Julie said, her voice steady and determined as she extended her hand expectantly. Just as she issued the first command, a sharp glint from an instrument caught the light. Stacy slapped it into Julie's palm with confident precision in a swift motion, the cool metal pressing against her skin, signaling it was time to work.

Two hours later, Julie peeled off her blood-stained gloves, the slick crimson remnants a stark reminder of the intense surgery she had just completed. With a practiced motion, she untied her mask, loosening the tight fabric that had pressed against her skin, and finally inhaled deeply, welcoming the fresh air into her lungs. Julie took great pride in her surgical skills, always striving to leave minimal scarring on her patients. Mr. White was no exception. The precision of her techniques ensured he would heal beautifully, a testament to her dedication and expertise.

"Another great one, Dr. Banks!" Stacy exclaimed as she entered the room and carefully removed her sterile surgical attire. "He's one lucky bastard," she added with a playful smirk, her eyes sparkling with admiration and excitement for the skillful work they had just accomplished.

Julie nodded thoughtfully, her eyes surveying the bustling scene as her medical students peeled off their crisp surgical gowns and engaged in quiet conversations. Throughout the intricate procedure, she had maintained a steady stream of dialogue with them, guiding them through the complexities of the case and addressing their probing questions about various medical techniques and protocols. She loved her role as a teacher and surgeon.

Before she could thoroughly remove her sterile surgical attire, a nurse rushed into the room, urgency evident in her eyes. "We've got a gunshot victim in the ER!"

Julie sighed, a sound heavy with the burden of her reality. Being on call entailed more than just staying late. It involved sacrificing her time, her rest, and sometimes even her sense of self as each hour blended into the next in the demanding world of trauma care.

Julie quickly stripped down and rushed to attend to the next patient, leaving her students behind. The group would catch up with her before the subsequent surgery. She needed water and a quick granola bar, which she ate while navigating the maze of halls to reach the ER.

After an hour of sleep in the doctor's lounge, Julie felt rejuvenated and prepared to tackle her on call rounds before heading home for eight hours of rest.

In the Intensive Care Unit, Julie observed Dr. Garcia engaged in a quiet conversation with the police chief. Their heads were leaned close together, a gesture that sparked an unsettling feeling within her. The intensity of their discussion made her heart race, and despite her efforts to dismiss it, she couldn't shake the unease arising from the chief's involvement in her patient's case. The weight of that connection lingered in the air, intertwining her professional concerns and a deep, personal discomfort.

"Dr. Banks," one of the nurses said, "Mr. White is awake."

Finally. Would he remember his question for her?

She mentally shook her head. How silly it was to think about that, of all things.

"Dr. Banks, wait a moment," Police Chief Ronald Wise said as he hurried after her. "I need to talk to that patient."

Anger ignited within her, a fierce blaze fueled by her protective instincts. She understood the police's need to interview her patients—those who had been victims of horrific crimes—but the urgency of their quest conflicted with her professional duty. At the very least, she believed she should thoroughly assess their mental and emotional states before allowing anyone else to pry into their suffering. "I'm not sure he's in a state to speak with you," she said, her voice steady yet tinged with compassion as she sought to shield the vulnerable from further harm.

"Oh, I imagine he's spitting fire by now," Chief Wise remarked with a chuckle, his eyes twinkling with amusement. Julie furrowed her brow, confused by the humor that eluded her.

"Do you know the patient?" she asked, her voice laced with curiosity and concern.

Chief Wise nodded, his expression serious as he stepped closer to her. They rushed down the busy hospital corridor toward the recovery room, where Mr. Rodney White was waiting. "You could say that," he responded cryptically.

As they entered the brightly lit room, Mr. White's eyes widened in astonishment at the unexpected sight of her standing beside the police chief. His expression hinted at a whirlwind of emotions, leaving her to wonder which had caught him off guard more.

"Mr. White, I'm Dr. Julie Banks, and this is Police Chief Wise. How are you feeling?" She took the stethoscope off her neck to examine her patient.

With a dazzling grin, Mr. White flashed a wicked smirk in her direction.

Before he could say anything, Chief Wise commented, "Hey, Doc."

Julie faced the imposing figure of the chief. Her brow furrowed in curiosity. "Yes?" they both responded.

She quickly glanced back at the patient, her eyes widening in disbelief. "You're a doctor?" she exclaimed, her voice filled with surprise.

Instead of giving a direct answer, he cleared his throat, his expression serious as he responded, "Doc, you owe me an answer to a question."

Chapter Three

DOC KNEW HE had shocked the doctor. Julie—he liked that name. It had a beautiful ring that lingered in his mind. He wasn't serious but wanted to see if she had a sense of humor, a spark of wit that could brighten his day. Strangely enough, he felt an inexplicable urge to engage with her despite their recent introduction amid the turbulence of the hospital environment. But damn, she was a striking woman. Tall, standing at least six feet. He could imagine her as a runner with her lean, athletic build. However, the baggy scrubs and oversized lab coat concealed the full extent of her physique, leaving her a tantalizing mystery yet to be unraveled.

A searing pain ricocheted through his back like a shockwave, and he couldn't hold back a low, desperate groan of anguish. The fading effects of the pain medication filled him with dread.

She skillfully dodged the question, just as he had done with her inquiry about being a doctor. "Let me examine you first, and then we'll arrange for some pain relief to alleviate your discomfort as you recover," she said, her voice soothing and professional.

Doc wanted to embrace his tough persona and stubbornly refuse the pain medication altogether. Still, he wasn't naive enough to overlook his ability to heal quickly. "Just light meds," he conceded.

As Julie started her meticulous examination, he glanced up at Chief Wise, who was watching him closely and with concern. "How's it going, Chief?"

"Not too shabby, Doc. Care to explain what the hell happened?" Wise's tone was sharp, yet it carried an undercurrent of concern.

A flicker of memory swept through Doc's mind like a shadow. "How's Simon?" he asked, dread slowly creeping into his chest.

Julie's hands froze briefly on him, her expression shifting to worry as the chief shifted uncomfortably. He knew the answer, and his heart sank further at the thought of Simon not making it after Doc had been so eager to invite his friend to visit.

"Dr. Garcia worked on him for five grueling hours, but ultimately, the extent of the damage was too severe…." Julie began, her voice trailing off as Doc raised his hand to interrupt her.

"I got it," he said, his voice laced with anger—not directed at her, but at the unyielding situation before them.

Simon had always admired and envied Doc's life: first, as the fearless paramedic rushing headfirst into danger; then, as a steadfast Navy SEAL team leader; and ultimately, as the compassionate protector, guiding civilians and military personnel through crises. This deep-seated envy may have fueled Simon's misguided belief that he could fend off an attacker with a sharp knife.

Exhausted, Doc wiped his hand across his tired face, weighed down by guilt. It was his fault, and the realization loomed over him like an unwelcome shadow.

Julie gently examined the tender wound on his back, her fingertips gliding across his skin, each delicate press eliciting a response that was a strange mix of pain and unexpected longing. What was happening to him? His friend lay motionless, the weight of guilt heavy on his conscience, yet here he was, his mind betraying him with thoughts of the doctor's skilled hands intimately exploring his body. He was in urgent need of help, both physically and emotionally.

"Everything looks good," Julie reassured, her voice calm and warm as she focused intently on the tablet before her. "I'll send in those pain medications for you right away. Once we're finished here, we'll move you to a private room, and if all goes well, you'll be on your way home tomorrow." She offered an encouraging smile, her eyes sparkling with genuine care.

Doc felt utterly detached from himself, the weight of his impending journey pressing heavily on his chest. The thought of returning to his empty home did little to comfort him. Before long, he would make his way to Kissimmee, Florida, to attend Simon's funeral. As he envisioned the sorrowful faces of Simon's family, a sinking feeling settled in his stomach—they would mercilessly blame him for their tragic loss. Deep down, he knew they were right. He shouldn't have taken Simon down that alley shortcut. He was all too aware of the lurking dangers that haunted the streets of Baltimore. The joy of laughter and camaraderie had clouded his judgment, and now he faced the bitter consequences of his choices.

Doc stared at the stark white wall ahead, oblivious to Julie as she quietly slipped away from his recovery room. A heavy silence filled the space, punctuated only by his faint voice, "Chief, can we do this later?"

Chief Wise stepped forward, his presence immediately filling the air with tension. "We can handle this later, Doc. But I need you to know that we caught the two who attacked you and your friend. As the police rushed to the scene, they were seen fleeing with bloody knives in their hands."

Relief washed over Doc like a fleeting wave in a sea of despair. This was good news. Yet, deep down, he felt an unshakable weight of sorrow. He nodded slowly as resignation and acceptance overtook him.

The chief reassuringly patted his leg before stepping back.

What should he do now? With his job suspended in limbo during his recovery, an unsettling, suffocating emptiness enveloped him like a thick fog. Work had always served as a sanctuary for him, a bustling escape that distracted him from the relentless, spiruling thoughts tormenting him like shadows in the night. Now, the vivid memories of his last moments with Simon flickered like a film playing in slow motion in the alleyway, surging forward and invading his mind with each painful heartbeat.

"Hello, Mr White," a nurse greeted as he entered the room. "I have some pain medication for you, along with another dose of antibiotics prescribed by Dr. Banks." Rodney nodded appreciatively at the young man who skillfully maneuvered a computer cart beside him.

How could he smile when Simon's laughter had been silenced forever? A heavy weight settled in his chest as memories rushed back, memories filled with the anguish of survivor's guilt. He had struggled with that deep-seated feeling during his years in the military, enduring countless hours of counseling after a harrowing overseas operation that had cost him part of his team. While he recognized that this wasn't the same brand of guilt that gnawed at him now, something felt far more unsettling. It was the burden of knowing that he had unintentionally taken Simon away from the world, a truth that shattered him to his core, pushing him toward the brink of despair.

Another male hospital employee entered as the nurse passed him the prescriptions and a glass of water. "I'm here to take him to a room," he announced.

"Thanks, Kevin. Just give me a moment and I'll walk you over. He should be heading to Room 312."

The other employee nodded with a slight smile. "That's what I have, too," he confirmed.

Usually, Doc would have been eager to ask probing questions and engage in meaningful conversations with the two individuals beside him. However, a heavy blanket of sorrow enveloped him, making it nearly impossible for him to initiate dialogue. He felt a profound indifference toward the mixture ominously pumped into his veins. His focus was consumed by the storm of grief raging within him. At that moment, all he craved was solitude, a chance to confront the profound loss weighing on his heart.

Matt Hamilton awaited him as he was rolled into the brightly lit confines of Room 312. As a fellow former SEAL team leader and co-owner of Hamilton Investigation and Security, Matt wasted no time. "The chief filled us in on the situation. How are you holding up?"

Knowing all the men at HIS, Matt would best understand his loss and how he compared it to military losses. Doc spoke the truth. "Shitty."

"I understand," Matt said, his voice steady yet laced with concern. "We can discuss it whenever you're ready. But tell me, how does the wound feel?"

Doc shrugged in a familiar gesture of indifference. "Fine, as far as I can tell." He tried to hold a brave front despite the throbbing pain.

"I imagine you want some time alone right now," Matt continued, his tone softening, "but the men found out about your stay in the hospital. I suspect they'll swing by to check on you at some point."

Damn it. Doc craved solitude but couldn't deny that the agents had good intentions. "Got it," he said, resignation creeping into his voice.

"Okay, I won't hold you up any longer," Matt said, his words hanging in the air. After a moment of silence, he continued. "Doc, I'm just a call away if you need me."

"Thanks, Cap," Doc replied, the shortened form of the military term "captain" flowing easily from his tongue, a reminder of their shared rank, history, and camaraderie.

Matt opened the door to find Cowboy with a pizza

box balanced in one hand. The aroma of melted cheese and spicy pepperoni wafted behind him.

"The food here will kill you," Cowboy joked, suddenly stopping as he recognized the weight of his words. "Sorry, man."

Doc nodded in acknowledgment, fully aware that Cowboy's comment was harmless.

As the hours passed, agents began to file into his cramped room, each bringing a delicious pizza to share. Laughter and chatter filled the air, the scent of freshly baked pies mingling with the sterile smell of the hospital. With so much food piling up, Doc directed some of the surplus to the nurses' station and the doctors' lounge, ensuring everyone could enjoy the unexpected feast.

As the men slowly departed, the quietness enveloped Doc like a warm blanket, bringing a wave of relief he had desperately craved. Yet, after only a few brief minutes of solitude, he felt restlessness creep in and called the nurses' station, his voice sounding even more fragile than he felt. "Would you ask the doctor if I can have something to help me sleep?" he inquired, his tone a mix of hope and defeat.

Deep down, he understood that true slumber wouldn't come to him as the weight of the night's events pressed heavily on his eyelids. Only the soothing embrace of medicine could coax him into a dreamless oblivion. Otherwise, he feared the relentless replay of the fight would haunt him throughout the night.

A bright presence entered the room before the nurse could fulfill his request for a sleep aid. Pup bounced in with cheerful energy, followed by their newest puppy trainee, Casey, who wore her adorable "Service Dog in Training" vest. Casey's tail wagged energetically as she sensed the shift in the atmosphere.

For the first time that day, a genuine smile spread across Doc's face, lighting up his weary expression. His heart swelled with affection for the dog. She embodied love and warmth, and her presence comforted him.

"I thought you might like some doggie kisses," Pup said. A wry smile danced on his lips as he observed Doc's demeanor change with the arrival of the beloved furry companion.

With the word "kisses," Doc's mind drifted back to the enchanting Dr. Julie Banks, her vibrant smile and sparkling eyes remaining in his thoughts. The mere anticipation of seeing her again made his heart race, filling him with excitement and longing.

"Yeah," Doc said, "I'd love for Casey to join me."

Chapter Four

JULIE SLIPPED INTO her coat and took her leather purse from the neatly organized locker in the doctor's lounge. Just as she was about to leave, her phone jolted to life, ringing insistently. She quickly pressed the device to her ear. "Dr. Banks."

"Doctor, Mr. White in Room 312 is asking for something to help him sleep," a nurse said, her voice tinged with concern.

Her heart raced at the thought of Rodney White, the embodiment of a patient who ignited a fiery enthusiasm within her. What about this individual made her blood surge with adrenaline and urgency? She mentally shook her head, acknowledging that this intense feeling stemmed from her fervent dedication to her work, the thrill of being the first on the scene, and her unwavering commitment to her patient's well-being—far exceeding the cautious recommendations of the physicians.

As the memories replayed in her mind, she couldn't shake the awareness that her instinct to act stemmed from a deep sense of empathy and an unyielding desire to make a difference. This pull was more profound than any conventional training could instill. It was not merely a physical urge.

"I'll drop by and talk to him on my way out."

"Thank you, Dr. Banks."

After ending the call, Julie removed her coat and draped it over her arm. She knew she could have prescribed a sleep aid for her patient, but she wanted to see Mr. White again before heading home. Once again, she reasoned it was purely from a physician's standpoint, not a woman's desire for a man.

As she exited the elevator on the third floor, she noticed the nurses clustered around Mr. White's room. Her heart raced as she hurried forward, eager to help in a medical emergency.

"What's wrong?" she asked, her authoritative tone honed by nine years as a trauma surgeon. Time was always critical, leaving no room for niceties in emergencies. One had to develop a thick skin to navigate the chaos.

The four nurses stood up and looked at her with shy smiles. One brave nurse grinned and said, "You have to see this, Dr. Banks. She's absolutely adorable."

Adorable? She first envisioned a child. Did Mr. White have children? She didn't even know if he was married. Although he wore no ring and hadn't asked for anyone, she concluded he was single.

Once again, she mentally shook her head to clear her thoughts. She shouldn't have entertained such thoughts about her patient. She was glad he would be released tomorrow, allowing her to refocus on her work.

As Julie entered the room, she spotted what the nurses had been raving about: a yellow lab puppy wearing a "Service Dog in Training" harness was kissing the cheek of the fifth nurse on duty. Upon seeing Julie, the nurse straightened.

Attempting to soften her tone, Julie smiled and asked, "What do we have here?"

The nurse looked taken aback. "I'm sorry, Dr. Banks."

She waved her hand dismissively. "It's no trouble, but I was requested to help Mr. White get some rest."

The nurses rushed out of the room, and Julie turned to Mr. White, raising an eyebrow. "If you wanted to ask a nurse out, you could have simply asked instead of interrupting their duties."

The young man beside the bed chuckled, grasping the puppy's leash. "Doc doesn't need help getting a woman."

Julie noticed "Doc" staring at his companion with an icy glare. "You can blame *him* for bringing the dog."

Kneeling, Julie let the puppy sniff her hand before she petted it. Soon enough, the puppy climbed onto her knee and started licking her face. Julie couldn't help but laugh heartily. She understood why the nurses were so eager to receive affection from the little one—it was soothing.

"Casey, heel," the man said. The dog paused her kisses, trotted back to him, and sat down, her tail wagging.

Standing and clearing her throat to reestablish her role as a doctor, she evaluated the data on the machine connected to Mr. White. Once composed, she looked at him and smiled. "What's this I hear? Do you need something to help you sleep? Is everything all right? Are you in pain?"

Her patient looked at her and smiled. "Nothing's wrong, Doc, but I'd like to get some sleep tonight." He glanced at the coat draped over her arm. "Were you leaving? I didn't mean to make you go out of your way for me."

Julie shook her head. "It's no trouble. I had to pass this floor to get to the parking garage." She assessed Mr. White before nodding. "I'll have something sent to help you sleep. Goodnight, Mr. White." She turned to his visitor and nodded at him, taking one last look at the adorable puppy at his feet.

"Before you go," Mr. White said, "you owe me an answer to my question."

Surprised, Julie turned to the side and tilted her head. *What question?* Then it hit her. *That question.* She shook her head. "I'm sorry, Mr. White, but I don't date or marry my patients. Still, I appreciate the lovely proposal."

Mr. White narrowed his eyes at her. "Well, there's nothing more to be done. You're fired."

Julie jolted at his words. This man must be delusional to think she would marry him after a near-death proposal from someone she didn't know. "If that's what you wish." She turned to leave the room, saddened by the turn of events.

"Hold on, Doc," the visitor said. "Casey and I will walk you out."

Julie walked to the door, a wave of shame washing

over her for wanting to visit her patient. Still, she sensed he was joking about the proposal and firing her. "There's no need."

"Nah," the man said, "she needs the practice."

Uncertain about what training the dog needed, Julie nodded and opened the door. The handler paused to allow her to exit first.

As they silently walked to the elevator, the nurses took one last look at the dog, even though they might have been admiring the handler. He was a handsome man, had a sexy appeal, while the puppy only enhanced his persona. However, Julie preferred her men to be more rugged, like Mr. White.

As she entered the elevator, the handler turned to her. "I'm Pup," he said.

Confused, Julie tilted her head in question. "Pup? I thought the dog's name was Casey." At least, that was the name he used when giving her commands.

He chuckled. "Her name is Casey, but they call me Pup since I'm the lead handler at the agency and the youngest agent."

Julie still had no idea what he meant, so she nodded, hoping to wrap up the conversation while her thoughts swirled around Mr. White.

"Is Mr. White a doctor?" she asked, puzzled about why this question came up first.

Pup shook his head. "Nah, he's a medic. He used to be a paramedic before becoming a SEAL. Now, he serves as a medic for one of the teams."

Agency. Teams. Where on earth did these men work? The government? It felt secretive, but she discovered Mr. White had been a SEAL.

They stepped out of the elevator and into the parking garage.

Pup cleared his throat. "You know he was just kidding, right?"

Once more, she found herself absorbed in his conversation. "About?" She looked around the lot, ever watchful for vagrants and potential attackers. Not that there had been any incidents since security started patrolling the lot every hour.

"Firing you, obviously." Pup chuckled. "He's just pulling your leg about the proposal."

"Oh." Julie couldn't understand why it bothered her that it wasn't real, even though she realized it was an impossible situation. "Does he do this often? Propose to women he just met?"

"Not that I know of. Doc is pretty particular. Given his size, he prefers his women tall and athletic." Pup chuckled again. "Just like you."

To change the subject, Julie asked, "How old is Casey?"

"Six months. She's still a baby learning but has so much potential."

"Where is she getting her training? You said you were the main handler. Where?" She needed to understand more about Mr. White, even though she didn't want to admit it.

"We're employed at Hamilton Investigation and Security."

Julie waited. He spoke as if she should know this agency, but she had never heard of it. "Is this in

Baltimore?"

Pup shook his head. "On the outskirts, we have a few acres for practice and planning. We even have an outdoor range."

Guns? She didn't see Pup carrying one. "You have a weapon?"

He nodded. "I'm just carrying a backup piece at my ankle. We don't typically open carry unless we're on the job. There's no need for it."

Julie reflected on the circumstances surrounding Simon and Mr. White's injuries and considered that a gun could have been a wise choice, though she kept that opinion to herself.

The parking lot was primarily empty at this late hour. On days she had surgery—long hours on her feet—it was her routine to rack up extra steps by parking as far from the exit as possible. She pointed ahead. "That's me. I can make it the rest of the way."

Pup shook his head. "Nah, let Casey practice. Besides, Doc would knock me senseless if I let you walk to your car alone."

Sighing in resignation, Julie gave in. It shouldn't take long. She'd love to see the puppy in action. She had never watched a dog check out a car before. "Okay."

"So, anyway," Pup said, as if they had been in the middle of a conversation. "At HIS, we complete missions that no one else can or will. We work for private individuals and the government alike."

Bewildered, Julie asked, "The government? Don't they have teams to handle things?"

Pup nodded. "They do, but sometimes the

government needs things done and can't get their hands dirty, if you know what I mean."

Julie, impressed by this organization, vowed to learn more about it. Although she might never need its services, it would be interesting to read about it. She stopped in front of the blue SUV. "We're here."

She watched in awe at the attention the puppy gave to her handler. It was as if no one else existed. When Pup instructed her to search the car, Julie stepped aside, observing the dog explore every nook and cranny around her vehicle.

After Casey was done, she sat and whined at Julie's SUV.

Pup reached for his weapon at his ankle. "Doc," Pup said firmly, "you'd better move away from the car."

A bit uneasy with his new authoritative tone and the brandishing of his weapon, Julie furrowed her brow and straightened her posture. "What on earth for?"

"Because," Pup said, "Casey just discovered her first non-training explosive."

Chapter Five

THE WORD "EXPLOSIVE" echoed ominously in Julie's mind, reverberating like a haunting melody that would not fade. Why would anyone harbor such a sinister desire to blow up her car? Or worse, to cause her harm while she was sitting inside it? A sudden chill crept down her spine, its icy fingers grasping at her heart as she struggled with the horrifying realization of how narrowly she had escaped a brush with death.

Numb at the thought, Julie allowed Pup to lead her away from her car. Once outside the garage, he pulled out his cell phone and called someone—she assumed it was 911. As he spoke, he typed on his keyboard faster than anyone she had ever seen. Meanwhile, Casey lay beside him, playing with a toy he had given her after the bomb discovery.

Julie rubbed her hands up and down her crossed arms. Questions kept running through her mind. Was it a fluke that it was her car? Did someone want to blow something up, and it worked since her car was parked alone at the edge of the lot? Or—she straightened.

That must have been it.

Doubting herself, she couldn't imagine Dr. Garcia sabotaging her car over a malpractice suit stemming from his negligence. No, that suit would move forward without her as a witness and remain intact. They understood the practice would struggle once he had to compensate the victim's family, and they had agreed to remain steadfast during the media frenzy and patient loss he would face.

"Doc," Pup said, pulling her from her thoughts, "is there anyone who'd want to hurt you?"

Julie shook her head, her voice trembling as she replied, "Not that I'm aware of."

"Well, you'd better think long and hard because the police chief will want to know the answer."

While hospital security chatted with Pup, Julie observed the controlled chaos around her. The bomb squad, what appeared to be the entire police force, and several men dressed in black who resembled mercenaries, had arrived. The controlled nature of the chaos settled within her. It felt like being calm, controlled, and precise in the operating room.

She couldn't sit back and let others take care of this for her. She needed to grasp the reasons and the people involved. When she turned to the police chief and Pup, she saw a shocking sight.

Mr. White stepped out of the hospital, dressed in all black like the other men who had arrived and stood to the side.

This was under her control, so she grasped and tugged the thread. She stalked over to Mr. White, narrowing her eyes. "You should be in a hospital bed. I don't want the stitches I painstakingly sewed to rip open because you needed to come out here looking all badass with your buddies."

He grinned at her. "You think I look badass?"

Julie huffed. "Is that really what you took from what I said?" She dug deep to maintain the calm that this man was quickly undermining. "Look, you don't have to stay here. If you want to leave the hospital, I can't stop you. But my medical advice is to stay tonight so we can make sure no blood clots have formed."

"Keep in mind, I fired you." Mr. White arched a brow.

Julie rolled her eyes. "I know that was a joke because of what I said about dating patients, so you can stop the ruse."

Mr. White shook his head. "I can't do that, Doc." He placed his hand over his heart. "You've captured my heart. I need an answer to my question. I know it's early, but we can make it work."

Julie muttered, "Of all the egotism and stubbornness, I get stuck with this one." She looked him in the eye. "No, I won't marry you. Does that end this nonsense?"

His smile radiated warmth into her chilled veins, melting away the icy tendrils of fear and bringing a comforting glow to her heart. She reminded herself that she couldn't fantasize about this man—she just couldn't. He was a patient, and she wasn't interested. *I'm not.*

"For now," Mr. White said. In all seriousness, he continued. "Tell me what's going on."

Shrugging, Julie considered why she felt the urge to share everything with this man. Instead, she went to speak with the police chief, leaving Mr. White and his friends behind.

"Hi, Dr. Banks," Chief Wise said. "I'd say it's wonderful to see you again, but these circumstances make it quite challenging."

She nodded. "Hi, Chief. What's happening?"

He glanced over her shoulder and nodded. Then, Julie felt a presence behind her. She turned to see a wall of black. The men with Mr. White had shielded her back as if anticipating an attack. Shaking her head in disbelief, she turned back to the chief.

"The bomb squad will take care of the bomb. Let's head inside and talk."

"Sure," she said, walking beside the chief, "but I'm unsure how I can help. I don't know anyone who would want to blow me up."

They entered the hospital and went to the security office on the first floor. Inside, the chief sighed, sat down, and took off his hat. "Have a seat, Dr. Banks."

The wall of black remained outside the door, except for Mr. White, Pup, and Casey. They stood to the side, leaning against a wall, while Casey continued to play with her chew toy. Its squeaking was the only sound in the room.

"Please, call me Julie," she said, sitting across from him at a round table.

"Julie, you can call me Ron. Now, young lady, tell me about anyone who might want to hurt you."

Julie shrugged once more, scanning the room full of men. "I have no idea."

"Okay," the chief said, "tell me about your patients.

Are any of them upset with you because of your work, or have any passed away while under your care?"

Instinctively, Julie shook her head and thought. "Of course I've lost patients. Some gunshot victims arrive too late or have sustained lethal wounds, making even my expertise unable to save them. But that's only three. It's been years since the last death occurred."

"Okay," the chief reiterated, "I'll need their names and any consequences that came from it. Is anyone threatening you? Are they considering suing?"

"I'll have my assistant gather the names and information for you. As for threatening, no." In the first part, she remembered that she didn't actually have an assistant. She relied on Dr. Garcia's assistant because she hadn't taken the time to replace her own after losing the last one to absenteeism. The two assistants were twins, and it felt wrong to replace one while the other remained behind.

"How is your practice going? Any lawsuits or threats?"

Julie cleared her throat and glanced at Casey and the puppy's joy. She wanted to smile but needed to stay stoic during this questioning session. She informed him about Dr. Garcia's lawsuit and how they had included the practice in the suit.

"Hmm. What are you testifying about in this case?" Chief Wise noted the family's name.

The Newmans lost their son when he was struck during a gang shootout. The child had been sitting on his front porch when the bullets hit his small body.

"As for court—nothing. I attended the surgery, but

Dr. Garcia led the procedure." She didn't mention that she believed Dr. Garcia might have skipped a step that contributed to the boy's death. She would reserve that for court. Moreover, it reflected how she would have performed the surgery—her opinion was not necessary since her method is just one part of a broader approach.

"Well, they might think you're taking Dr. Garcia's side. Have there been any updates from the family?"

Julie couldn't imagine the lovely family trying to kill her simply because she might side with her partner in their lawsuit. That seemed a bit extreme.

"How's your partner? Any problems with him?"

There are many, but Julie wasn't going to discuss all of them right now. "The usual stuff."

Chief Wise tilted his head and raised his eyebrows. "Just the usual stuff. Keep in mind, I'm not a doctor."

Julie felt as though she was betraying confidences by discussing her issues with Dr. Garcia. "Well, some surgeons have a god complex, and Dr. Garcia is one of them."

"You don't have one?" Chief Wise raised an eyebrow in disbelief. "A god complex?"

Julie shook her head with a sincere expression and replied, "No. I'm only human."

With his pen poised above his notebook, light reflecting off its surface, the chief leaned forward, his curiosity evident. "Okay, tell me about these usual problems."

"The ongoing lawsuit has caused considerable tension in our relationship. However, it hasn't reached a point where he would genuinely contemplate ending my life."

Ignoring the conversation's last few words, the chief maintained a commanding presence and asked, "What else?"

"He wants to bring in another partner, but I'm still considering my options," she replied, her voice steady despite the tension.

"Why not?" His brow furrowed with curiosity.

"Because it's a surgeon just like him. I don't need more hardheaded men trying to navigate the tumultuous waters of our work together," she explained, her tone tinged with frustration. She glanced at Mr. White, memories of her hushed words about his unwavering stubbornness flickering through her mind like a candle's flame.

"It must be incredibly challenging for a woman to navigate a male-dominated field," Chief Wise remarked.

Julie felt the weight of those words settle on her shoulders, a familiar burden she carried daily. She replied with a slight nod and a resigned expression. "It is."

"I hear you're likely the next pick for chief of surgery. Are other surgeons eyeing the position, maybe feeling envious that you appear to be a shoo-in for this esteemed role?"

She wondered how the chief had already encountered that gossip, especially since she had only learned about it earlier. "The only person I knew considering entering the fray was…." Her mind raced with the implications of the competition ahead.

The chief narrowed his eyes. "Let me take a wild guess: Dr. Garcia, your clinical partner. Are there any other issues I should be aware of with Dr. Garcia—maybe office politics?"

Julie nodded and discussed the minor things that regularly happen with her partner. Nothing serious, but considering everything, including her potential selection as chief of surgery, it became clear that this had to be it. There was an undeniable sense of finality in the air as if all the events had culminated in this very moment. Everything pointed to this conclusion, leaving no room for doubt.

Chief Wise scanned the dimly lit room, his sharp gaze drifting over Julie's shoulder. "Doc?" he called, his voice steady and authoritative.

Julie glanced up, prepared to reply, but was interrupted by Mr. White's voice cutting through the tension. "Yeah, Chief. We've got it."

With deliberate movements, the chief stood, his stature commanding attention. "All right, Julie. Please stay away from Dr. Garcia until I sort out a few things. Doc and his team are going to help protect you, just in case Dr. Garcia, or whoever dared to plant a bomb on your car, makes another move."

"What do you mean they're going to protect me?" Julie asked, her heart racing and eyes wide with concern and disbelief, as if she had just been told that the earth was flat.

"It means," Mr. White replied, a hint of mischief dancing in his grin as if he were letting her in on a thrilling secret, "screw your doctor-patient rules. We're about to be more friendly than you ever expected."

Julie gulped, feeling the weight of his words pressing

down on her like a heavy blanket. Two thoughts swirled in her mind, each more troubling than the last. First, they believed she needed protection. Maybe, just maybe, protection was justified since the discovery of the bomb. Second, this arrangement would draw her closer to Mr. White than she had ever wanted. He unsettled her with his smug demeanor, yet a curious desire to understand him better tugged at her conscience, battling against her strict code of ethics.

Taking a deep breath, she stood from her chair, gripping the table's edge as if it could anchor her in this turbulent moment. "Is there another way?" she implored the chief, her voice unwavering despite the storm within.

"No. I don't have the manpower for protective custody, but these men do. Trust them. Doc will make sure you're taken care of," he said, his tone allowing no argument, yet the finality in his voice only heightened her unease.

Him taking care of her was what worried her the most.

Chapter Six

DOC WAS IN pain, yet he stubbornly refused to admit it. This was the same surgeon who had once miraculously saved his life, and now, in a twist of fate, she needed saving. It wasn't every day that one had the chance to repay a doctor with actual services—a rare opportunity to return the favor in the most meaningful way possible.

He turned to the team in the hallway, specifically to one of the leaders, Grits. He didn't offer any apologies, knowing the men were ready to fight whatever demon dared to enter their realm. Doc understood he should defer to Grits but couldn't shake the feeling that he should lead this operation. Once Grits gave him a slight nod, he realized he had the green light.

"Right," he said. "Grits, Pup, check her place out. Be thorough, Pup. If Casey can't handle it, contact the police department for backup."

Pup, looking offended, stood tall. "Oh, she's ready."

Doc nodded and opened his mouth to continue giving orders when Julie tapped him on the shoulder. "Excuse me," she said.

Doc turned his full attention to her. "Yes?"

"Take a look at my house? What's wrong with it?"

"Maybe nothing, but it makes sense that if they planted a bomb here, they could've done the same at your place."

Fear flickered across her beautiful face, and a knot tightened in Doc's stomach.

"Oh," was all she said.

He turned to face the team and noticed the group pairing before him.

"We have the Newmans," Cowboy said, standing beside Ballpark.

"We've got Dr. Garcia," Nemo said, with Joe Stone beside him.

"We're with you on the detail," Boss said, along with the last few new agents that Doc hadn't had time to meet.

Realizing there was nothing left to arrange, he turned to Julie. "Doc, we're going to investigate this for you and keep you safe until we know what's happening and who has targeted you."

"What if the target is the hospital and not me?" she asked, hope shining in her eyes.

Three figures dressed in dark clothing approached the group, yet Doc couldn't help but grin.

"That's for our team to decide," Jesse Hamilton said, walking alongside his brothers, Matt and Brad. "Sorry we're late to the party, Doc."

He reached out and shook his big bosses hands, each giving him a nod of encouragement.

Doc said, "You all know what to do, team. Let's get

started."

"Devon is ensuring the safe house is prepared in case you want to use it," Jesse said to Doc.

As he looked at Julie, Doc realized she wouldn't want to hide away and avoid working. Given the safe house was in Virginia, she would likely decline their protection offer. "I think we'll keep it local. She's going to want to work."

Julie flinched. "I can speak for myself."

Doc was starting to admire this woman. At first, it was playful teasing, but now he respected her courage and dedication to her patients. He raised his eyebrows. "All right, then go ahead and tell us."

Taken by surprise, her lips moved in disbelief. Then she shook her head. "I'm not sure what's happening here," she admitted.

Doc glanced at the group as they quietly dispersed. "Let's head back inside and talk about this," he suggested to her.

The chief nodded and exited the room as they entered, leaving the two alone. "What don't you understand?" Doc remained standing, aware that sitting would only exacerbate the pain in his back. He'd hold off until he had no choice but to attempt it.

"You need to rest," Julie said as she got comfortable in her seat. "Now, let's pretend I'm a patient, and you're the interpreter for the doctor. Break it down for me in simple terms."

Doc knew she wasn't uninformed, but he wondered if the explanation and the delay in leaving had helped ease her nerves. "Okay, someone planted a bomb in your car."

She dropped her shoulders and sighed. "Not that part. I mean this protection deal you agreed to with the chief."

He believed hovering over her might not help her relax, so he gradually settled into the chair as a fire shot up his back. He seethed, and Julie's eyes narrowed.

"It's fine," he reassured her. "Just unexpected," he lied.

Julie pursed her lips as if struggling to keep her words in check—probably something he wouldn't appreciate.

"Well, as you mentioned, we aren't completely certain whether the hospital was the target or if you specifically attracted the danger. I owe you my life, so I'll make it my mission to ensure nothing happens to you."

She flashed a bright smile that could light up even the dullest of rooms. "You know, most people just settle the bill."

Humor provided a refreshing touch amidst the gravity of their situation. She would need that humor, especially if she were the intended target, as a killer doesn't typically stop at the first obstacle in their path. "Well, I'll leave that to the insurance companies. This is now deeply personal."

"Do you really believe it's me they want?" she asked, her voice trembling slightly. This revealed vulnerability as uncertainty painted her features like a shadow.

Doc shrugged casually, though his expression remained serious. "It was your car. It might have been a crime of opportunity, a chance taken in the inky darkness, but it was quite far from the hospital."

"I enjoy walking," she asserted, her tone stronger now.

With a teasing smile, Doc raised his eyebrows in playful disbelief. "You mean you don't get enough exercise in that sprawling hospital?"

Frowning, she replied, "Sometimes I spend long hours standing in surgery, so stretching my legs is a simple pleasure."

He initially thought she was a runner, but perhaps she was more of a walker. Either option would keep her in shape, and she looked incredibly fit to him. Perfect, in fact.

Doc shook his head. "All right, you have two options. First, we can stay in a safe house in Virginia while everything is investigated to ensure your safety. Alternatively, we can stay close by, and you can still work."

She smiled at that, but Doc raised his hand. "There are a few restrictions."

Julie narrowed her eyes. "What kind of restrictions?"

"You can't go anywhere without one of us accompanying you."

Julie leaped from her seat. "That's impossible. I need to meet with patients, and I can't violate HIPAA just because you think I need a chaperone. Besides, I need to perform surgery, and I'm not letting anyone who isn't part of my team in there. Lives are at stake."

Doc stood up slowly, stifling a grunt of protest. "Your life may be at stake, too."

She sank back into a chair with an exasperated sigh. "What if I just go home and return to my normal life?"

The worry that she might actually do that occupied Doc's mind. "I guess you could, but I thought you were smarter than that."

"Do I truly have a choice?" She looked up at him, her striking blue eyes full of concern.

Doc nodded. "You do, but understand that this is our work, and we excel at it, so you'll be safe with us."

Julie slapped the table and stood up. "Then I choose to work. Where will we stay? Can we stay at my house if they don't find a bomb there?"

They were making progress now.

"No," he said firmly, the tension in his voice evident. "That would make it far too easy for them to find you."

"Won't my working do the same?" she asked, a hint of defiance in her tone, raising an eyebrow as she crossed her arms.

Doc nodded slowly, his expression serious. "Yes, which is exactly why you have two options: the Virginia option for when you need safety and our option of closely following you. We'll make sure that nothing jeopardizes your safety."

"Why are you going to such lengths for me? I didn't ask for protection."

With a broad smile, Doc remarked, "Because you didn't provide me with a satisfactory answer to my question."

Julie laughed, and Doc's heart leaped at the joyful sound. "I still won't marry you," she said.

"We'll see," he joked. "Now, let's get moving. Oh, I have a request."

Julie chuckled and tilted her head. "Oh, at last, a request instead of a demand?"

"Just call me Doc."

"But you aren't a doctor."

So, Pup had caught her up on his past. That big-mouthed kid. "It's what the others call me."

"Won't it be confusing if they call me Doc?"

He paused for a moment. It would be, but it wouldn't stop the team. He would know when they intended him and not her. "Okay, you may call me Rodney."

She extended her hand. "It's nice to meet you, Rodney. I'm Julie."

His large hand enveloped hers, and they shook as if he didn't already know her name. A jolt of electricity shot up his arm, catching him off guard. He quickly withdrew his hand and cleared his throat to conceal his blunder. "Ready?"

Julie rubbed her arm and nodded. "I'm ready." She stepped toward the exit, then paused to turn back. "What about clothes, toiletries, and other essentials? I'll need those from my home."

"Grits is collecting them for you."

She stopped, and anger laced her words. "What? Someone is rifling through my personal things?"

"Of course," Doc said, shrugging as if it were no big deal. He never understood why women were so sensitive about men picking up their things when men typically didn't care who collected their belongings as long as they were gathered.

Julie muttered something under her breath. Doc caught the phrase "pig-headed" during her tirade, but just smiled. She appeared to have returned to the woman he had met before. Good. She'd need that strength if someone were targeting her.

Rodney studied her momentarily, a glimmer of amusement flickering in his eyes as if he had just seen an unexpected lab result. "Every good doctor knows when to call it a day. I think it's time to leave the hospital." He opened the door for her.

As they exited the room, Rodney raised his hand, his finger slicing through the air to carve a command circle. Instantly, the men lounging against the walls snapped to attention, their movements precise and synchronized as they formed a tight circle around the two of them. The atmosphere thickened, charged with eerie tension that felt surreal and electric, as if time paused in their moment of gathering.

They approached two imposing black SUVs quietly. Led by Rodney, Julie slid into the back seat of the first vehicle while Rodney settled in beside her.

Julie laughed nervously. "I have my own entourage."

"Hell of a way to get it," one of the new guys remarked, and Doc shot him a furious glare.

As they pulled away from the hospital parking lot, the sounds of the city fading behind them, she realized he hadn't answered about where she would be staying.

Julie fidgeted in her seat. "I don't remember where you said I'd be staying. Which hotel?"

Doc turned to her. "No hotel. You'll be staying at my place."

"The hell I am."

In an instant, Doc realized she was the woman for him.

Chapter Seven

JULIE COULD HARDLY wrap her mind around the audacity of her patient trying to pull the strings of her life. The very idea of staying at his house? Outrageous! She imagined the scene: her, a complete stranger, thrown into the chaos of this man's home, mingling with a bunch of unfamiliar faces—men she had only just met. It bordered on the ridiculous. How did he expect her to waltz into that circus? No way. Not happening! A mix of disbelief and frustration bubbled within her. Surely, there had to be another way out of this madness. Deep down, her favorite fantasy flickered to life: perhaps this was all an elaborate hoax, a cruel joke.

Caught in a whirlwind of panic and disbelief, she desperately searched for another way to face the day ahead. A day that had turned into a waking nightmare. A bomb in her car! How could this happen? It had to be a mistake—a cruel twist of fate. She fervently thanked God for having the foresight to let Casey inspect her vehicle before she dared to approach it. The chilling thought of what might have occurred had she turned the key and unleashed that deadly engine sent shivers down her spine. She could almost feel the explosion reverberating through her mind, a haunting reminder of just how close she had come to oblivion.

Frustrated with what her life had become, she snapped, "Go to your home? No way, Rodney!"

He raised an eyebrow, a teasing smirk appearing. "Why not? It's as secure as a bank vault on lockdown."

Seriously? Did this guy crawl out from under a rock? "Because I don't know you from a hole in the wall."

Rodney shrugged, a playful glimmer in his eye. "Guess what? I don't know you, but I'll risk my life for you."

"See, here's the rub. I don't want anyone risking their life for me, especially people I don't know." She shook her head in disbelief. "This feels like something out of the Twilight Zone."

Rodney chuckled. "Twilight Zone? When did blowing up cars become a feature of the Twilight Zone?"

She wanted to stomp her foot to emphasize her point but knew she had to act maturely to win this battle. "You know what I mean."

With a heavy sigh, Doc wiped his hand across his face. She could see the pain in his eyes from the wound she had just repaired. She realized it must be painful for him to sit like that.

"I get that," he said. "I really do. It's a difficult situation for anyone to deal with. And maybe we'll find out that only your car—not you—was the intended target, letting you move on and leave all of this behind quickly."

Julie could only hope for a resolution, but she didn't

want to believe that the hospital had become the target of a sinister plot either. The thought of her colleagues and patients being harmed was unbearable. How did her life spiral into this chaos? She has always been a law-abiding citizen, following the rules—except for the occasional red light she ran while responding to emergencies at two in the morning when the roads were clear. She has nurtured strong friendships and treated them with care and respect. So, when did she become unworthy of peace? Surely, she deserves better than to have her world turned upside down.

She stiffened her back and tried to take control of the situation to prevent herself from breaking down. "Let's revisit this and see what other plans can be implemented."

"Is there a reason my house is so offensive?" Doc shifted in the seat, and she could only hope he hadn't torn the stitches she had painstakingly placed.

"I don't—" She cleared her throat. "I don't find your place offensive. I—" Julie wasn't sure how to explain this to him. He seemed so eager to take on a job he thought needed to be done for her, while she just wanted her life to be simple and straightforward. "It's just a lot to take in all at once."

Rodney nodded. "I get that, too. However, as you would in an operating room, you must take this seriously. No matter the circumstances, you must take charge and do what's best for your patient. Here, you should prioritize your well-being so we can protect you until we're sure you aren't the intended target. After that, we can reassess the situation. If everything checks out, you can say goodbye to us. But I won't allow you to dismiss me or the team until I determine it's safe."

Julie's back tensed as her anger flared. Of all the things to say when she began to understand his perspective. "You won't? What do you mean, 'You won't?'"

He winced. "I guess it was the wrong choice of words."

Her blood ran hot. "You guess?"

Rodney flashed that cocky little smile she was beginning to appreciate. "Are you going to repeat everything I say?"

Refocusing herself, Julie shook her head. "No. I need to take control of my life. I can't just hand it over to a stranger."

"Okay, how about we partner on this, then? We'll do as you wish—" Rodney raised his hand when she opened her mouth to speak. "—to a point. We won't do it, or we'll make other arrangements if I think it's unsafe. Can we agree on that?"

It didn't seem like she had many options in the matter. This man and his teammates genuinely believed she was in danger and wanted to protect her. Her! A complete stranger. Now, she was truly repeating herself. At least he was seeing things her way and compromising. She realized she had no alternatives. Those men would follow her around until they decided it was clear or got bored playing superheroes.

With a sigh, she replied, "I can work with that. But only until we determine if the bomb was meant for me, which I seriously doubt since I haven't made any enemies in my life."

"You'd be amazed at how many enemies one accumulates without even realizing it."

"I doubt I have any. I try to be respectful to others, but sometimes it leaves me at a disadvantage."

Rodney furrowed his brow. "In what way?"

She sensed her words had struck a nerve. While she meant what she said, she hadn't intended for him to take it so seriously. "I appreciate the little courtesies in life, like letting others move ahead of me in line. However, when this happens, it often delays my plans more than I expected. It's like my experience in traffic. Those small gestures can significantly disrupt my timing."

"What about Dr. Garcia? Have you made an enemy out of him? With the trial and everything?"

Despite the whirlwind of emotions in her heart, she and Dr. Garcia upheld their professional camaraderie. They rarely crossed paths in the office, often occupied with patients or tied to their respective hospital duties— sometimes even on opposite shifts. To her surprise, he hadn't treated her any differently since the incident. But was he truly okay with her testifying at the trial? Sure, the medical board cleared him, but did that mean she should also feel free?

Yes, she felt a twinge of blame for him, but it was only because she would have handled things differently. Yet, did that make her right? After all, her choices could have also led to the boy's tragic fate. Perfection was a tall order in her field. One misstep in her line of work could result in bitter enemies and lost lives. The pressure was immense, and she felt the weight of it all teetering on the edge between duty and morality.

"I don't think so. Our professional relationship has remained as steady as a heart rate monitor during a code blue," she replied, her playful yet resolute tone resembling that of a surgeon in the operating room.

Redirecting the conversation, she said, "Where's your home? What kind of place is it? How many bedrooms does it have? Where will I sleep?" Her curiosity overwhelmed her sense of propriety.

Turning to her, Rodney offered a small smile. "Inner Harbor," he began, his voice steady and reassuring. "It's a townhouse with three bedrooms. You'll be in one of the guest bedrooms. Does that answer your sudden barrage of questions?" His tone was both teasing and informative, cutting through the tension of the unknown.

Julie felt a heat wave wash over her at her unexpected reaction to him. The way he smiled, with a playful glint in his eye and the teasing lilt in his voice, wrapped around her like a warm blanket, accompanied by his commanding presence. Not to mention how strikingly handsome he was, with his chiseled jawline lightly shadowed by several days of stubble and short hair that fell just right. But she knew she couldn't allow herself to think that way— not now, and certainly not ever. He was a patient, and the strict code of ethics dictated the boundaries she must uphold. She didn't have any genuine desire for him. She merely found him—her mind raced to capture the right words. It came to her with sudden clarity, like a snap of her fingers. She found him "undeniably charming," enchanting in a way that tugged at her tightly held composure.

With a nod, she replied, "Yes. Thank you." She

didn't ask where he and the other men would sleep. She had no intention of bunking with any of them, no matter how real the threat might be.

When her cell rang, she nearly jumped out of the car. Pulling it from her purse, she saw Laura calling on video. As she went to answer, her mind raced with thoughts about what to say. "Can I tell my friends where I'm staying?" Not that she knew.

Rodney shook his head. "Nobody."

She planned to revisit that point later but wanted to respond now in case it was urgent, as Laura usually didn't call during Julie's work shift. She accepted the call and positioned the phone so she could see her face on the video call. "Hi, Laura. Is everything okay?"

Her friend's voice came alive on the phone. "Okay?" she asked. "I just heard there was a bomb at the hospital. Are you okay? Of course, you're okay. I see you."

Julie wanted to laugh but knew it wouldn't be well-received, so she replied, "You're not going to believe the day I've had." That was all she could say before Rodney reached over and ended the call.

"Hey! I was talking to my friend." How could he end her call without her permission?

"No one knows where you're staying, what happened today, or anything about us. If you'd like me to be your shadow, you can introduce me as a visiting colleague so I can go with you everywhere in the hospital."

Still furious over his disconnecting her call, Julie narrowed her eyes at him. "Hell no, I'm not."

Chapter Eight

DOC REALIZED HOW much he'd angered Julie, but he couldn't allow her to tell her friends everything and jeopardize the one advantage they had—surprise. No one would suspect she had personal protection. Yes, he'd likely gone too far by ending her call, but he knew she was about to disclose their location and destination and that he was with her.

He ran a hand through his short hair, trying to maintain his composure. "Look, I'm sorry. I should've fully briefed you before you took the call."

She raised an eyebrow, and her face flushed. "You think?"

Okay, he'd crossed the line. It was important to understand his limits. "I'm sorry. You can only talk about what the news organizations and the hospital say. You can't reveal that the bomb was in your car or that you're under a form of protective custody."

Crossing her arms against her chest and unknowingly pushing out her luscious breasts, Julie huffed. "It's beginning to sound more like a prison."

Doc chuckled. "Some say that." But as reality sank in, his expression turned somber. "But you know what? They're alive to say that."

A heavy pang of guilt slammed into his gut like a sledgehammer, the weight of regret almost unbearable. *Simon.* Simon was gone. Doc's heart twisted at the thought of his friend's absence. He should've chosen their route differently and spared Simon from the fate that encountered him that horrific night. Doc had navigated that alley countless times without a hitch, yet in that moment, all he could see were the shadows of his failures. He should have protected his friend and not gotten caught up in the reckless bravado of a kid trying to make a name for himself in a gang initiation. The knowledge that he didn't save Simon clawed at him, leaving a haunting echo in his mind: How could he ever promise to safeguard someone else if he had let his closest buddy down?

As if feeling the tension in his body and recognizing the seriousness of his expression, Julie said, "I'm sorry, Rodney."

He straightened his posture and cleared his throat. "While it may feel restrictive sometimes, I want to assure you that it's not a prison sentence. As long as we can maintain safety, you can continue with most aspects of your normal life. Either I or another agent will accompany you during this period."

"Will I be able to talk to my friends at all?"

Sensing her need to involve her loved ones, Doc decided it wouldn't hurt to ease her worries. Since she would be out and about, seeing them wouldn't pose a problem if they could ensure adequate security. "We'll see," was his gruff response.

As if on cue, her phone rang insistently, piercing the tense atmosphere. Doc turned his gaze toward Julie, a mix of hope and anxiety swirling in his chest, praying she would make the right decision. He dreaded the thought of ending another call, fearing it would drive a wedge between them and breed resentment in the woman he envisioned could one day stand by his side as his wife. Had he really allowed such thoughts to enter his mind? Marriage? Not at this moment, but he could undeniably picture a future where they were together, forever intertwined. Something about Julie resonated within him. Perhaps it was the intense attraction, that undeniable spark igniting his senses, yet he suspected their connection ran far deeper than lust. There was an unbreakable bond between them, a genuine intimacy he had never encountered with any other woman before.

Julie held his gaze, and while he couldn't read her emotions, he could've sworn he detected a hint of lust from her before she assumed her professional mask. She glanced at her phone, silenced the ringer, and placed it in her purse. Then, she returned her gaze to him with a pained expression that he interpreted as fear and despair. Unlike him, who had just lost a friend, Julie only had her friends on hold, so the despair didn't fit. Yet he wouldn't second-guess what he'd seen. He'd figure her out before long.

As if sensing that she needed reassurance, he nodded and turned back to the front. Doc wondered if he should have chosen the safe house in Virginia and not given her a choice instead of his small home. It was big enough for a few people, but the team might make her feel overwhelmed in the house. On the other hand, he would have had to hogtie her to pry her away from her patients, even for her own safety. He loved her unwavering dedication.

Yet, he worried he couldn't protect her if she went out in public. Sure, they had protected public figures before, but none had recently faced a bomb attached to their vehicle like Julie had. The hospital would be safe, but if someone wanted Julie to pay for something, they would have to follow her home. Coming and going wouldn't be easy since he lived in an area with street parking and no assigned spaces. They'd be vulnerable for too long if they couldn't secure parking nearby. He needed to devise a solution because he wouldn't let anyone hurt Julie.

By a stroke of luck, two spaces were available near his home. After parking, the group from the second vehicle joined them, and the four men did as Doc expected—they formed a tight circle around him and Julie. The only issue was that he and Julie were tall, which might require reconsidering the protection detail. A new agent—about five feet ten inches tall—brought up the rear. This would be his last day on this detail.

When the team entered his home, they did a quick sweep—not that he anticipated any trouble since his security system was still active—to prepare Julie for what lay ahead.

"Will they do this every time?" she asked, nodding toward the two men heading up and down the stairs to check it out.

"Sweetheart, they'll do this everywhere."

Her back stiffened, and she narrowed her eyes. "Absolutely not in my patients' rooms! They won't tolerate it. I won't allow it."

Doc truly appreciated this woman's spirited nature. She was a firecracker, and he anticipated their vibrant banter. "Of course not."

After entering, Doc showed Julie around and led her to the room where she would sleep. It was across from his, which reassured him. He liked knowing he would be nearby if she needed anything. Of course, he couldn't imagine what she might need that would require him to leap out of bed to provide. Sex, maybe?

He pushed that thought out of his mind. She was a client, and clients deserve his full attention. *Just like Simon should have....*

"When will my bags get here? I'd like to shower and change out of these scrubs."

Just then, a knock echoed at the front door, followed by a dog barking. With a smile, he gestured with his thumb over his shoulder. "I guess that's them."

"We'll order dinner tonight. What are you in the mood for?" he asked, while listening to the men below. It was indeed Pup, Grits, and Casey. Doc was curious if they had found anything at Julie's home, but he wanted to give her his attention.

"I believe I deserve some comfort food."

Finally, a woman who confidently expressed her preferences without resorting to dismissive phrases like "I don't care" or "You choose." He found someone who understood her thoughts and articulated her desires with clarity and conviction. "I know the perfect place," he said, his eyes sparkling enthusiastically. "I'll send you the link with the menu after I grab your clothes."

He hesitated, reluctant to admit that he found her scrubs particularly endearing. They were a simple shade of blue, the fabric unadorned, yet they hugged her figure in a way that beautifully highlighted her curves, making her look effortlessly polished even in such a casual outfit. He could only hope her regular clothing was as appealing.

After descending the stairs, he updated the men on their dinner choices and took the bag Grits offered. "Is there anything urgent?" he asked, eager to ensure the bag reached Julie promptly. Who was he kidding? He was genuinely looking forward to seeing her again so soon.

Grits shook his head. "Nothing that can't wait."

Doc nodded and then went back upstairs to Julie. "I trust they packed everything well. If there are any shortcomings, please make a list, and I'll ensure they gather those items tomorrow."

She took the bag from him, smiled, and said, "Thank you," then shut the door in his face. He chuckled. *Oh yeah, getting to know this woman will be quite entertaining.*

Back downstairs, Doc and Grits huddled together in the kitchen while the men kept watch or slept in the spare room. He had installed bunk beds in that room for his young nephews' visits to the big city. Although it didn't happen often, he wanted them to be as comfortable as possible during their stays.

"Someone tried to break into her house. There are wedge marks on the front and back doors. She has an impressive lock system. She needs a security system to go along with it." Grits shrugged. "Anyway, that was it. She's a neat freak. Everything was in order."

Doc imagined that anyone requiring precision and meticulousness in their work would also be orderly and organized in their personal life. He believed that everything had its designated place, and that was where it belonged.

During dinner, Pup continued his nonstop chatter about dogs. "Did you know this about dogs?" "Did you know that about dogs?" Typically, Doc could put up with it, but tonight, he wanted to talk to Julie more, to engage her in front of the group and observe her reactions. Someone meant to be his wife needed to handle the guys while they were working, not as if they were two different people. One was tough and standoffish, while the other embraced life because they understood it was a gift.

After clearing the disposable dishes, Julie asked, "What time do we leave tomorrow? I need to be at the hospital by five a.m. I have two surgeries scheduled before I do rounds."

Doc scheduled a time that suited her, and then she nodded and went back upstairs for the rest of the evening. He didn't like the quiet Julie he'd noticed during dinner and afterward. It felt as if she were accepting this like a prison sentence. Maybe the men had been too aggressive and scared her. Damn Pup and his endless chatter.

They had tomorrow to nurture the deep, meaningful relationship he envisioned. He would also have the chance to observe her skills firsthand, for she would never enter the surgical room, surrounded by others deftly wielding sharp instruments, without his protective presence.

No. Initially, she would resist, but excitement flared within him when Jesse called to inform him that the hospital administrator had permitted him to shadow her throughout the building. The thought danced in his mind, and he couldn't help but smile, knowing how much she would dislike the surprise. He was determined to find that spirited woman once again. One day, she would look into his eyes and say "Yes" to the question he'd posed during their first meeting.

Chapter Nine

DARKNESS SCOURED THE area when they left Rodney's home. Julie was accustomed to the hour and felt energized by her schedule. The two SUVs blocked the street, waiting for her and Rodney to enter. When their hands accidentally brushed against each other, electrical currents surged through her. She gritted her teeth. *He's a patient.*

While Julie primarily specialized in trauma surgery, she performed several general surgical procedures. Today, she was scheduled for both a hernia repair and a bowel resection, procedures that required her expertise to ensure optimal patient recovery and minimize complications. As usual, her mind focused on the day's events, and the drive blurred by until the hospital came into view. At that point, she became antsy and eager to start her day. She would consult with the patients in pre-op, reminding them of what to expect and check that her staff and students were accounted for to avoid any issues.

Stacy encountered her in the women's locker room in the surgical wing. "What's happening? You didn't return my calls last night. I was worried sick when I heard about the bomb scare here. I'm relieved I was already home, but I knew you would probably still be at the hospital."

After speaking with Rodney the night before, she clarified what she could share with everyone, including her friends. It annoyed her, but she understood. "I'm sorry. A friend came into town last night, and we were catching up for most of the evening." She closed a locker that contained her personal items. "I didn't mean to worry you."

Julie was amazed that the men had concocted cover stories in such a short time. She nearly went ballistic when Doc told her he had been approved to shadow her this week. While he prepared in the men's locker room, one of the men kept watch outside the women's locker room. And yes, they had swept the area before she could enter. It felt like too much, but Julie wouldn't let her focus waver from her patients and the procedures she would conduct today. She would handle the rest this evening because Mr. Rodney White would hear from her.

"Did you notice those hunky guys in all black walking around? The nurses are curious if there's a high-profile patient today." Stacy raised her eyebrows in playful teasing. "Wouldn't that be exciting?"

Julie sighed. Yeah, it would be great if they followed someone other than her. "Listen, Stacy, do you remember Mr. Rodney White? He was the man I recently operated on."

Stacy smiled. "Who could forget that hottie? Why?"

Licking her lips, she tried to stay focused on the

story. "Well, he's a medical colleague, and the hospital has permitted him to shadow me for a few days because he may want to switch to trauma surgery."

"Oh." Stacy furrowed her brows. "Is this who you were with last night? I mean, he's a patient and all, but if he's a medical professional too…."

Julie straightened her back and told her friend another lie. "Of course not. He may be a colleague, but he's still a patient."

Stacy tapped her finger on her chin. "Now that I think about it, didn't he fire you? Would that make him fair game?"

Rolling her eyes, Julie walked toward the exit. "I'll see you in surgery." She then left while Rodney, dressed in scrubs, waited for her at the door.

"Is everything all right?" he inquired.

Julie sighed as she walked. "I really hate lying to my friends."

"It's just for a little while. We might find out today that you weren't the target, and you'll be free from us."

Why did she suddenly hesitate to embrace her freedom from Rodney? It felt as if she had only just exchanged weak introductions with him. Yet, he had already shown himself to be an overwhelming presence, a blustery brute whose impact was impossible to ignore. There was something attractive about him: a hot, rugged charm and an intimidating demeanor that kept her entranced. He had many admirable qualities, revealing his depth and a disarming smile that made her weak in the knees. But still….

"Hmm…Let's get the day underway."

Their first stop was the bustling pre-op area, a hive of activity filled with the low murmur of anxious voices. With her warm smile and reassuring demeanor, Julie checked the charts on her sleek tablet, her fingers gliding effortlessly across the screen. After a quick review, she approached her first surgical patient, a young man sitting on the edge of the bed, his eyes wide with apprehension. Julie paused to kneel beside him, making direct eye contact and absorbing the tension that enveloped the room. She cherished these moments, observing her patients' expressions—some eager, some fearful, but all reflecting their hopes and anxieties about the procedure ahead. With a calm and soothing voice, Julie offered gentle reassurance, and gradually, the man's taut shoulders relaxed. Her goal was to alleviate their fears and instill a sense of anticipation for the positive transformation that would follow once they awoke, free from their ailments.

After consulting with Jonathan Nelson about the herniorrhaphy, she led Rodney to the surgical suite, where she introduced him to the surgical team and carefully prepared for the operation. The surgical attire, aseptic scrubbing, and hair containment were vital for maintaining a sterile environment. Any deviation from these protocols could lead to postoperative infections in the patient following the procedure's incision.

As she entered the surgical room with Rodney close behind her, nerves overwhelmed her. She had only experienced this level of anxiety during her early surgeries when she was new to surgery. Now, she was a pro—an esteemed surgeon with countless procedures to her name—and this was merely a simple hernia repair. She could perform it in her sleep. However, with Rodney on the edge of the room, scrutinizing everyone present, she felt as if she was facing her very first surgical trial.

Trying to push him from her thoughts, she turned to her students. Ryan, Darlene, and even Marla were there. She needed to ask them questions and forget he was nearby. It felt like a school instructor continuously supervised her work, even though he was there for her safety. However, she couldn't understand safety from whom in this room. And how could they get away with anything in such a big hospital?

"Miss Rollins, I'm glad you could join us," Julie said, pausing by the patient after passing the student. "Could you outline the steps we'll take today with Mr. Nelson?"

Marla blanched. "Well…" She hesitated. The student would fail the class if she didn't step up and study.

Julie turned to Darlene. "Miss Lang, could you explain, please?"

As the student described the standard procedure, Julie focused on the task at hand. She was in her element and her world. With Stacy by her side, she flawlessly performed the hernia repair and sent Mr. Nelson to recovery. She planned to visit him after he woke up and once she was on rounds.

"Great job, Doc," Rodney whispered to her as they exited the surgical room. They took off the protective clothing they had worn and washed their hands.

She felt proud. Though she knew feeling pride in herself was inappropriate, she couldn't help but sense that she had earned it when she received his approval. "Thank you."

"Next?" he asked, opening the door to the hallway for her. They stepped out, and she again guided him to the pre-op room.

"We're on our way to see Ms. Rebecca Taylor. She needs a bowel resection. We'll check in with her in pre-op and then get ready for the surgery." With thoughts of her impending procedure, she effectively ignored the man next to her.

"Do you do this all day?" he asked, interrupting her thoughts about Ms. Taylor's surgery plans.

Julie nodded. "Pretty much. Later, we'll make the rounds. I'll introduce you to my patients and see if it's all right for you to sit in."

Doc stopped and took her arm, turning her slowly to face him. "We may have removed the procedures for searching the patients' rooms before your arrival, but you will not enter a room without me. Am I clear?"

The sternness in his voice made Julie feel uneasy. She understood his words but had to consider HIPAA regulations. It was their choice if a patient didn't want a stranger to attend their medical visit. Typically, hospital patients were agreeable to this, but she couldn't be sure. She would have to wait and address the issue if it arose. She hoped it wouldn't, as she doubted she would win this battle.

Rather than voicing her opinion, she nodded and chose the easier route. "Whatever you say."

Rodney narrowed his eyes and examined her closely. "What game are you playing?"

She laughed. "Game? I'm playing the prisoner and doing what my warden tells me." She pulled her arm free from his grasp and turned to walk away. She knew he'd catch up to her quickly, but it felt good to assert herself—even just a little.

By the end of the day, Julie felt both fatigued and exhilarated. Her surgical procedures had been successful, and all her patients were showing positive signs of recovery after surgery. She saw that as a win for everyone.

After her outburst, Rodney remained silent as he followed her. This was somewhat unsettling, but it allowed her to focus on her work instead of the pointless chatter some residents engaged in while collaborating with her. All her patients allowed him to visit, even asking him medical questions, which he answered skillfully. It impressed her.

Yes, he had impressed her, even though she hadn't wanted him to. She had hoped he would fail so she could ask for another agent to accompany her—someone knowledgeable in medical terminology and procedures. But he had won her over. On that course….

That desire was creeping into her soul. Julie knew the attraction she felt was mirrored in the glances he gave her when he thought she wasn't looking. But she felt powerless to act on it. Or could she? Stacy had made a valid point about him firing her—whether he joked or not. But where did ethics stand regarding a former patient? She'd never explored this because she believed that once a patient, always a patient. Then she reminded herself it wasn't the Marines.

What she needed to focus on—instead of the handsome man beside her—was why they hadn't cleared her as a potential victim. Oh, she hated that word. But it would have applied had she started her vehicle. And when would the police return her car? Another thing to consider that had no bearing on the present moment.

As they settled into the backseat of the SUV, Julie turned to Rodney. "Why are you still protecting me? I thought you said you could clear me today." That had been her hope, at least.

He turned to her and shook his head gently. "I apologize, but we couldn't clear you or the hospital today. So, you'll remain in our care for at least another day until Jesse and his brothers determine if the hospital is the intended target. We're uncertain because neither you nor any personnel have received threats or experienced unusual incidents. We believe it's wise to prioritize safety in this situation and err on the side of caution."

A heavy weight overwhelmed her, as if the world's burdens pressed down on her shoulders. Surely, she mused, it couldn't be her they had in mind when discussing a potential explosion. It must have been the hospital they were referring to. Yet, despite this thought, an unsettling idea lingered—what if she had been the unfortunate casualty? The mere prospect of her fate could unleash a spiraling nightmare not just for herself, but for everyone within the hospital's walls.

"What's the problem?" Rodney asked, flashing that irresistible grin—the one that made her heart do a little dance. "Aren't you a bit charmed by me?"

And there it stood: the conundrum!

Chapter Ten

"DID YOU KNOW there are about four hundred fifty dog breeds out there? However, only around three hundred seventy of them are recognized by kennel clubs," Pup exclaimed, his eyes sparkling with excitement.

Doc sighed, feeling the urge to strangle the kid. Sure, he understood the handler's love for dogs, but seriously—was that all he could talk about? Casey, that adorable pup, lay curled at Julie's feet, looking like she was his entire world. Doc had reached his limit. "Hey, Pup, don't you think it's time to recheck the perimeter?"

With a bounce, Pup was up on his feet, and so was Casey, both eager to jump into action. "Absolutely, Doc! We're on it."

After the agent and dog exited, Doc turned to Julie. "I'm sorry about that."

She laughed, and it touched his soul. "It's okay. He's excited and a little obsessed."

Doc nearly snorted while laughing. "You could say that."

Julie let out a loud yawn, her body arching gracefully

as she stretched her arms high above her head, her chest thrust outward, undeniably drawing Doc's gaze. He cleared his throat, feeling a mixture of admiration and discomfort, and quickly averted his eyes.

"It's been an exceptionally long day. We need to go over the plan for tomorrow's trip to the courthouse," he suggested, his voice steady despite the flutter in his chest.

With a reluctant sigh, she let her arms fall to her sides, and Doc noticed a noticeable change in her demeanor—it was as if the air around her had become heavier. "I almost forgot about that. Is there anything different from today?" she asked, her brows furrowing slightly, revealing her worry.

"Not really, but we don't have approval to carry our weapons in the courtroom," he replied, a hint of frustration in his tone. The rule bothered him, yet he respected it to maintain good relations with the police chief and law enforcement. They worked in a close-knit community where stepping on toes was avoided at all costs.

"Does that matter? I mean, won't I be safe in the courtroom?" Julie asked, her expression marked by concern, her eyes wide and searching.

Doc snorted softly, the sound escaping before he could hold it back. "You'd think," he muttered, quickly realizing he had unintentionally added to her worries. "Yes, many officials will carry weapons. But you'll still ride with us and stay close, just like when we went to the hospital. We'll leave at zero eight hundred sharp," he reassured her, his voice softening as he tried to alleviate her anxiety.

Julie nodded, then sprang to her feet, throwing a playful salute like a soldier in a drill. "O'eight hundred sharp!" she declared, her tone teasing as if addressing a no-nonsense drill instructor insisting on a quick retort. With a mischievous smile dancing on her lips, she pirouetted and made her way toward the stairs leading to her room—the one that had Doc crossing his fingers, hoping she'd call for him any night of the week for any reason.

Doc wiped his weary face with a hand. Boy, oh boy, did she get to him—just that small, playful gesture stirred something inside him, warmth he hadn't anticipated. That little unexpected joy endeared her to him even more, making him realize how deeply she touched his heart. So, he'd have a wife with a vibrant sense of humor and lively feistiness—a combination he found utterly irresistible. Life was good, he thought, as a smile crept onto his lips despite his fatigue.

Before he could follow her to see if she needed anything, a knock echoed on his door. Cursing, he approached it and let Jesse, Brad, and Matt inside. The men filled his living room with their larger-than-life personalities. The brothers, who had founded and managed HIS, were rarely involved in cases. That's why it meant so much to Doc that they stepped in on this one.

After distributing the cold beers among the group, they found a comfortable sitting spot. The sun had set, but the moon cast a warm glow over everything. Jesse, leaning back slightly with a relaxed smile, broke the silence and asked, "How's everything going with you all?"

Doc shrugged. What answer was he supposed to give? That he didn't believe she could be the target because who would have anything against such a fantastic and caring woman? Or that he needed more time with her to persuade her that she would ultimately be his? Finally, he said, "Good."

Jesse lifted an eyebrow and smiled. "Hmm. That's impressive, huh?"

"I'm not quite sure what you mean, but yeah, there's nothing new to report. What about you? Have you narrowed it down to the hospital?"

Rubbing the back of his neck, Brad said, "That's the rub. We haven't been able to figure that out. As far as we can tell, the hospital wasn't the target, which leaves Dr. Banks."

Doc sighed as he gazed up at the ceiling beneath Julie's room. He found himself deeply torn between the urgent need to protect Julie from the looming threat posed by a sinister madman and the desire to cherish the precious, fleeting moments they had shared throughout that day. Every laugh, every glance, and every whisper felt like a thread woven into the fabric of his heart, making it even more challenging to consider letting go, even for her safety. At that moment, he was painfully aware that he wasn't ready to relinquish the warmth and joy their time together had brought him, especially when danger might be so close.

For the next hour, Doc and the Hamilton brothers gathered around the cluttered table, poring over every scrap of evidence they had collected on the case. The atmosphere was thick with frustration as they sifted through the details, their brows furrowed in concentration. They ultimately reached a sobering conclusion: they knew almost nothing that could help solve the mystery. Yet, Doc's unwavering determination cut through the uncertainty, compelling them to stay the course. They would remain vigilant, guarding Julie like sentinels until a clue appeared that would guide them in a new direction.

As Doc bid them goodnight, he glanced up the stairs and noticed Julie sitting on the top step, her head buried in her hands. A wave of concern washed over him. How much had she heard? Were there any words exchanged that might have unsettled or frightened her?

"Julie," he said softly, his voice infused with an unsettling calmness as he approached the steps, climbing to a position just below her. He sat sideways, his gaze searching her face intently, eager to gauge her reactions. "How much did you hear?"

When she finally looked up, a deep ache pierced Doc's heart. Her expression conveyed utter devastation, as if her entire world had crumbled into nothingness. "Enough," she whispered, her voice trembling with raw emotion.

He gently reached up, his fingers brushing against her soft cheek as he wiped away a single tear that glistened there. "I'm truly sorry," he murmured, his voice filled with sincerity and regret.

"So," she said, stifling tears. "It's really possible I was the intended target, that someone actually tried to blow me up."

Doc cringed as her words lingered in the air. Although he didn't appreciate how she expressed her concerns, it didn't lessen the truth behind them—a truth he couldn't ignore. He refused to lie to her. There was no reason to do so, especially when she was a formidable woman capable of facing any challenge.

"With someone attempting to break into your home on the very same day, it's a legitimate concern. Yes," he affirmed in a serious tone.

"How will we know when I'm safe? I mean, what if they never try again? Will you stay by my side forever?" Her voice trembled slightly, exposing the vulnerability beneath her strong facade.

He intended to be by her side forever, but not in the role she envisioned. He would be her husband one day, but this wasn't the right moment for that discussion. She wasn't ready for such a leap. "If necessary," he replied, his voice steady and honest, promising his commitment through his words, even as uncertainty lingered in the air.

"What did I do wrong?" she asked as another tear rolled down her cheek.

He longed to pull her into his arms, feeling the warmth and comfort it would bring, but he knew this conversation was too important to avoid. If he held her tight, the words might slip away from him. "It's possible that some madman has targeted you, perhaps simply because you're a tall woman or an exceptional doctor. The reasons can be as confusing as they are terrifying. But I promise you this: we will dig deep, and I won't rest until we uncover the truth before it's too late. You have my word on that."

Julie studied him intently, making him squirm under her piercing gaze. She knew he hadn't saved Simon, and this realization must have sparked doubt about his ability to protect her when the moment truly arrived. How could she trust him now?

Realizing he needed to end this conversation before it went too far, he stood up and extended his hand to her. "Come on. It's time to get some sleep. You have a big day tomorrow."

She nodded and took his hand, getting to her feet with his help. "Thank you, Rodney. I'm not sure I've mentioned it, but I appreciate your support in this matter."

"Well," he said, "I owe you."

As they walked toward their separate rooms, Julie turned around and smiled. "Like I said, most people just pay the bill."

Doc realized she would be okay if she could joke after everything she'd heard and their conversation. Now he had to keep her safe from an unknown threat. It wouldn't be the first time HIS had been in that situation. In fact, that was generally the case, but they had no leads to go on. Even the police hadn't found a signature on the bomb that would point them toward a specific criminal. They were almost at square one, and he didn't like it.

"The check is in the mail," he said with a smirk, an eyebrow raised in playful challenge.

She chuckled, shaking her head as she turned toward her room. "You don't know how many times I've heard that line. Goodnight, dreamer."

"Goodnight, Julie," he whispered to the closed door, a secret smile playing at the corners of his mouth. "Goodnight, my future wife."

Doc underwent a profound and unexpected

transformation: from a wild bachelor to a man enchanted by this woman's captivating beauty, ready to do anything to win her heart. This change was truly remarkable.

"My, how the mighty have fallen," he heard Pup comment from the bottom of the stairs, the truth hanging heavily in the air.

Doc looked down, narrowing his eyes at the agent, sensing the weight of unspoken vulnerabilities. How could he correct the kid when every word rang true? At that moment, the stakes were high. If anyone found out about his feelings for Julie, they would likely intervene, pulling him away from her. That was unacceptable. He resolved then and there to be her unwavering protector, her shadow until the time was right when he could confidently step forward and claim the role of her partner for life.

"Find something productive to do," he told the agent, then turned abruptly and stepped into his room. With a wave of emotion, he held back the urge to slam the door, instead shutting it firmly and quietly behind him, reflecting the strength of his resolve.

If he couldn't hide the chaos of his emotions from a naive, inexperienced kid, how in the world could he keep up that facade in front of seasoned agents carefully trained to notice even the most minor details?

Chapter Eleven

JULIE'S ATTORNEY CONTACTED her during her commute to the courthouse, reminding her that any statements made could have serious repercussions for her and her legal representation if the family proceeded with their lawsuit. This thought weighed heavily on her mind, leaving her in deep contemplation. Could this be the motive behind the attempted detonation of her vehicle? Was this an effort to prevent her from providing testimony? The question lingered, even as she considered that her testimony would not have any groundbreaking implications, regardless of its direction.

"Gun!" A piercing scream erupted from the front seat, shattering the tense silence. In an instant, chaos ensued. She felt the sharp crack of glass exploding around her and a searing sting igniting on her left arm as panic engulfed her while Rodney pushed her into the seat, shielding her body with his like a human barricade. At the same time, the SUV lurched forward, the engine roaring as it accelerated.

"Get us the hell out of here," she heard Rodney yell to the driver—a man he referred to as Boss—as if the agent needed direction. From what Julie sensed, that was precisely what he was doing.

"Are you hurt?" Rodney asked, pressing his body close to hers protectively.

She attempted to shake her head but couldn't move it because he had covered her. "I—" she said, terrified for her life. Someone had just shot at them. Or, rather, they'd shot at her.

"Christ, you're bleeding," Rodney said as he pulled away from her. "Let me see." He grasped her arm and turned her toward him, leaning in closer to examine— what, exactly?

"Change direction. Head to the hospital," he told the driver. "Julie's been hit."

Had she been injured? Did he mean she'd been shot? Why couldn't she— "Ouch!" she screamed, the sound bursting from her lips when Rodney's fingers grazed a tender spot on her arm. A sharp jolt of pain radiated through her, and she finally recognized the sting. How serious was it? Her heart raced as anxiety clawed at her insides, and she wondered how much damage had been done.

Taking a breath to steady herself, her medical persona took over. She gently moved Rodney aside. "Let me see."

Rodney raised his hands in surrender, leaning back while keeping his eyes on her. "Okay."

She turned her arm to get a better look at the wound. She had no idea a bullet wound could hurt this much. It brought tears to her eyes, but she fought them back. *Trauma surgeon,* she reminded herself, stiffening her spine. She could work through the pain. No, she couldn't repair the damage herself. She'd need someone else to do that, but she could examine the injury.

Unable to see the other side of her arm, dread gripped her heart as she realized she couldn't assess the full extent of the devastation. There was no exit wound to be found, no sign to guide her through the horrific uncertainty she faced as she examined the injury with trembling hands. The pain was relentless. Agony coursed from her arm, racing through every bone in her body like wildfire. She felt a deep, aching sympathy for the patients trapped in their suffering, waiting for surgeries that seemed to stretch into a cruel eternity, with no hope of relief from the torment of their pain.

Considering medication, she said, "There's some ibuprofen in my purse. Would you please get it?" It may not help much, but it was better than nothing.

Doc bent down and grabbed her brown leather purse from the floorboard. He sifted through it until he found an over-the-counter bottle of ibuprofen and handed her two tablets. Casper, the agent in the passenger seat, reached back and, after twisting off the cap, gave her a bottle of water.

With her left arm securely pressed against her torso, she accepted the medication from Rodney, tossed the pills into her mouth, and then took a sip from the water bottle to wash them down. The pharmacologic effects would likely manifest later due to their proximity to the hospital. However, starting the treatment reassured her about her healthcare.

"How serious is it?" Rodney asked, concern written

all over his face.

"Bad," she replied. "The bullet is still inside." She gripped her injured arm, bent at the elbow, pressing it tightly against her body as if trying to shield it from the world. A searing pain enveloped her senses, clouding her mind and overshadowing all her thoughts. The harsh reality crashed down on her like a tidal wave—she had been shot, and it felt surreal, as if her life had become a haunting nightmare from which she couldn't wake.

"It won't be long. I can see the hospital," Boss said from the driver's seat. "ETA is two minutes."

Julie nodded, not fully agreeing but acknowledging they were close, which was good because she was on the brink of passing out from the pain. She focused on preventing shock, aware that it could be possible if medical assistance didn't arrive soon.

As they screeched to a halt at the emergency entrance, Rodney opened the door before the SUV stopped entirely. Boss jumped out of the vehicle and opened her door. "Careful now," the agent said as he helped her from the SUV.

Rodney was by her side before she had fully stepped onto the concrete driveway. "I've got you," he said, holding her other arm to steady her.

"Good. Because I'm unsure if I can—" Then it went black.

When Julie woke, she discovered she was in a hospital bed with Rodney sitting beside her, watching her intently. He jumped up as soon as her eyes opened. "You're awake!"

She nodded as best she could, but a searing pain

ripped through her arm, stealing her breath and blurring her vision. Hadn't they seen her yet? Why were they turning a blind eye? She didn't want special privileges, yet this was a time of desperation. Trauma cases were rare during the day, only emerging as shadows at night when the gangs roamed freely, leaving chaos in their wake. "Wa—" Her dry mouth prevented her from finishing the word.

"Oh." Rodney grabbed a glass of water from her bedside. "Here." After she drank hungrily, he set the cup down and walked to the door, flinging it open. "Tell Sanders that she's awake."

He hurried back to her bed. "The doctor will be here soon."

Julie knew better. Typically, the nurse saw patients first, followed by the doctor, as it was standard medical protocol. "Have they removed the bullet?" She couldn't tell, as her arm felt aflame.

Rodney nodded. "Yes, the surgery was successful."

That's why he called Dr. Jeffrey Sanders, the trauma surgeon on call that day, since she and Garcia were scheduled to appear in court. Thank goodness their hospital had top-notch professionals.

To her surprise, Dr. Sanders and a nurse entered the room.

"How's our patient?" he asked with a smile, a stethoscope hanging around his neck and a sleek tablet in his hand.

"It hurts," she said as she attempted to sit up, but instinctively used her arm, causing a jolt of pain to shoot through it. "Ouch!"

Dr. Sanders reached for her while the nurse checked the machines and medications flowing into her system. "Take it easy. I don't want you to mess up my work that soon. How would it look if I failed on our future chief of surgery?"

Since the rumor started that Dr. Ryland Macon, the current chief of surgery, wanted her to replace him, her life changed. The other surgeons began treating her differently. They went out of their way to assist her, complimented her, and consistently showed her deference. It was unnerving.

"Come on," she said, adjusting the blanket with her right arm. "That's just a rumor."

Dr. Sanders shook his head. "If you say so. Anyhow, how's the arm?" He set the tablet on the end of her bed and pulled the stethoscope from around his neck.

"Hurts," was all she said as the cool metal of the stethoscope grazed her skin just above her heart. "Hey."

The doctor winced and pulled the instrument back. "Sorry." He warmed the tip with his hand and then said, "Take a deep breath. You know the routine."

She followed her doctor's instructions, taking deep breaths until he was satisfied.

"Let me see the wound." Dr. Sanders unwrapped the bandage and examined the area around the stitches, causing Julie to jump and let out a yowl. He looked at her with sympathy. "Sorry."

She jerked her arm away and rubbed the area she could without pain. The stitches looked excellent to her, and she would have minimal scarring. "They look good," she told the doctor, and she could have sworn he grew two feet taller with her compliment.

Releasing her arm, Julie looked up at the doctor. "Thank you. But could I have something for the pain? Something mild?"

Dr. Sanders nodded. "That's what Regina is doing right now."

When Julie glanced at the nurse, she saw her inject something into her IV line. She could only hope it wasn't a powerful sedative. "When can I be released?"

"I'd like to keep you overnight, but I know you. We'll hold you for a few more hours until the anesthesia has completely worn off so we can ensure there are no complications. You know the drill."

She did. The availability of ICU rooms also depended on the length of stay, which meant there was space for her to recover a bit longer. She appreciated this since she wasn't sure she could walk yet.

"Any questions?" Dr. Sanders wrapped the stethoscope around his neck and picked up the tablet to start typing.

She wanted information about the surgical procedure but decided to wait to review her medical chart for now. Currently experiencing residual sedation, she preferred to extend her rest. As a result, she gently shook her head and closed her eyes. "No, I'm stable and comfortable."

Dr. Sanders gently patted her leg. "Just let me know if you need anything. I'll be back in a couple of hours."

Although she didn't see them, Julie knew the doctor and nurse had left the room. That left her with Rodney, and the men she believed were outside her door.

"How are you, really?" Rodney asked, reaching for

her hand and surprising her.

She slowly opened her eyes, blinking away the haze that clouded her vision, and locked her gaze onto his wounded eyes—suffering yet searching. "I'm fine," she lied through clenched teeth, the words rolling off her tongue like bitter ash. Deep down, she felt a pang of guilt, fully aware that this painful moment was not just for her but was carved deeply into his heart. She could sense the weight of the injury she bore—his responsibility, his anguish—looming like a heavy shadow over them both.

With their hands clasped, Julie felt uncertain about its meaning. Was he offering her comfort? Why had he taken her hand in the first place? She was his client, and he was her patient. Neither relationship allowed for such a personal gesture.

Sensing her distress over his move, he released her hand and quickly stood, running his fingers through his short hair. "I'm so sorry." He turned to her, and she could see the pain radiating from his gaze. "I should have been sitting on that side. I should have been watching the windows more closely. Christ," he said, turning back to her. "I should have protected you."

"Rodney, I'm fine. This is nothing," she lied. "Just a scratch." A scratch that hurt like hell and would prevent her from doing her job properly.

The realization hit her all at once. She wouldn't be able to perform surgical procedures. Although the impairment was temporary, the thought of being unable to operate was overwhelming. Initially, her arm would be in a sling, significantly limiting her range of motion. While rehabilitation would eventually restore function to her arm, performing surgery would be off-limits for an indefinite time—until the chief of surgery decided it was appropriate for her to resume her duties, allowing her to transition from patient care to instructional responsibilities in the operating room, where she would guide her students through surgical techniques.

She took a deep breath, fiercely reminding herself that she was alive, and that was truly all that mattered. His despair pierced her heart as she looked at Rodney, filling her with an urgent need to lift him from that darkness. With a gentle touch, she leaned over and placed her hand on his, letting warmth and reassurance flow between them. "It's really okay, Rodney. You and the team did an incredible job. You got me here, and I'm truly fine," she said, her voice steady yet full of compassion, hoping to dissolve the shadows lingering in his eyes.

At that moment, a wave of dread washed over her as she realized that her ethical principles were being tested. Deep down, she prepared herself for the inevitable failure. Yet, surprisingly, instead of feeling guilt or regret, she experienced a strange thrill bubbling within her. Curiosity ignited her spirit, and she looked forward to the challenge with unexpected excitement.

Chapter Twelve

WHEN JULIE STIRRED again, the dim light of the hospital room revealed Rodney and the stern-looking agent named Boss huddled in the corner, their heads bent close together as they spoke in hushed tones, a palpable tension hanging in the air. The moment their eyes met hers, they abruptly stopped their conversation, the sudden silence amplifying the beeping of the machines surrounding her. Rodney, his expression a mix of concern and urgency, approached her bedside while Boss quietly slipped out of the room, leaving an unsettling atmosphere in his wake.

"What's going on?" Julie asked, her voice filled with confusion and concern as she tried to push herself into a sitting position, pressing against the sheets with only her right arm. The effort proved futile, and she let out a frustrated sigh, convinced that the task was simply impossible. Instead, she turned her gaze toward Rodney and asked, "Could you please bring me another pillow from the nurse's station?" Almost instantly, however, she changed her mind. "Never mind. Just get Dr. Sanders in here as soon as possible. I need to go home," she insisted, feeling the weight of her discomfort pressing down on her.

Rodney nodded thoughtfully, his brow slightly furrowing. He walked slowly to the door and opened it just enough to reveal a faint silhouette outside. They exchanged a few hushed words, the details lost to the quiet of the hallway. After a moment, he returned to her side, the warmth of his presence enveloping her like a comforting blanket.

He gently reached up, fingers brushing her cheek as he tucked a few rebellious strands of hair behind her ear, his touch tender and reassuring. His dark eyes searched hers for signs of discomfort, and with a soft, genuine smile, he asked, "How are you feeling?" His voice was low and soothing, filled with concern and care.

His tender touch—one she knew she should resist for the sake of her principles—sent exhilarating shivers cascading down her spine and wrapping around her toes, which she eagerly embraced. There was an undeniable allure about him that resonated deep within her soul. This gentle caress conveyed more than words ever could, whispering sweet nothings of his affection for her.

She swallowed and nodded against the pillow. "I'm okay."

As if he suddenly understood what he had done, Rodney yanked his hand away and quickly sat in the chair. "Good. You'll be able to go home now. Grits and Pup brought you a fresh outfit."

"Weren't they in the SUV behind us? What happened to them?" Panic gripped her heart as she realized she hadn't thought about their small caravan. The image of the tail SUV facing the shooter filled her with dread, especially after Boss had floored the accelerator, leaving them all in a race against time and uncertainty.

Every second felt like an eternity as fear gnawed at her insides, wondering if they were safe.

"They're okay. They pursued the SUV that fired at you but lost it in city traffic. Red lights and everything."

A shiver ran down Julie's spine as the horrifying truth settled in—the shooter was still out there. Fear tightened its grip around her heart, each beat a reminder that her life hung precariously in the balance. Desperation clawed at her mind as countless questions raced through her thoughts, but the most agonizing of all remained unanswered: why was this nightmare happening to her?

Before Rodney could elaborate, Dr. Sanders entered with a warm smile. "Good afternoon, Dr. Banks. It's comforting to see you awake. How's your arm? Are you feeling any lingering pain?"

As Julie's mind danced between thoughts and emotions, she noticed a persistent, throbbing ache that pulsed through her arm—an ache she felt was manageable, a testament to her resilience. Tentatively, she moved her arm, bracing for the sensation. A sharp twinge of pain flared momentarily before it subsided, leaving her with a lingering awareness of her body's fragility.

She wouldn't have said anything if it hurt at all because she was ready to leave the hospital. "Everything seems normal. I'm ready for discharge."

"Understood. I'll begin the discharge documentation process. In the meantime, a sling will be applied to support your arm for several days until you can move it more freely without pain. Additionally, a physical therapist will visit to provide you with specific exercises designed to maintain strength in your arm."

Julie nodded, having anticipated this process and often recommended it throughout her career. "Thanks,

Jeffrey."

More somberly, Dr. Sanders said, "Julie, I hope you can outrun whatever is after you. I heard about the bomb, and now this. Please take care of yourself."

A thick, heavy knot lodged in her throat, constricting her breath. She desperately avoided the horrifying memory of the bomb attached to her car, the chilling connection between that explosive threat and her current predicament hanging like a dark cloud over her. Reality was relentless, no matter how much she wished to bury her head in the sand. It was serious—someone was determined to see her dead.

Clearing her throat with a slight rasp, she said, "Thanks." Her voice was barely above a whisper. She nodded slightly as Dr. Sanders exited the room, his calm demeanor and reassuring presence leaving her to her thoughts and unease—and Rodney.

As Julie waited to be discharged, Stacy and Laura hurried into the room and rushed to her bedside.

Laura embraced her. "Stacy called me as soon as she found out you were in surgery. How are you? What happened?"

Stacy pushed Laura aside and then bent down to hug her as well. "Chill, Laura. Are you okay?" she asked Julie.

A loud throat clearing caught Julie's attention. "I'll be outside if you need me," Rodney said before stepping out of the room.

She watched him leave, convinced they had experienced a breakthrough and could possibly consider themselves friends. Yet, her current friends wouldn't allow her to dwell on that now. They were eager for details.

Laura deferred to Stacy. "You take the seat. You're on your feet all day while I sit behind a desk." As a medical billing and coding expert at a medical practice, Stacy spent all day sitting, which she hated. She often tried to persuade her employer to buy a standing desk to improve her leg circulation, even though there was no real issue with them.

Stacy sat and nodded at Laura. "Thank you." She then turned to Julie. "Are you okay?"

Julie's heart swelled with gratitude, tears threatening to spill as she felt the overwhelming warmth of her friends' thoughtfulness. Their urgent presence in a moment of chaos spoke volumes about the depth of their care. "I'm fine," she whispered, trying to suppress the emotions surging within her.

"Is that sexy guy in your room the one you told us about? The one who's been your shadow for a few days?" Laura beamed. "He's hot. You should hit that."

Julie raised her eyebrows and smiled. "Hit that? What are you, sixteen?"

Laura fidgeted. "It's what the young women at work say."

"Well, I'm not going to *hit* that. He's my bodyguard, and that's all." Julie couldn't believe she had said "bodyguard," but it was true. There was no point in hiding it any longer. The shooting brought everything to light.

"So?" Laura asked, arching an eyebrow. "Haven't you seen that movie with the bodyguard?"

Stacy rolled her eyes, clearly unimpressed. "Yeah, but do you remember how it ended?"

Laura sighed, her confidence faltering. "Oh, right. So, what happened today?"

Julie hadn't talked with Rodney about what she could and couldn't share with her friends, but she wouldn't hide the truth about this situation, which made her feel better. She hated lying to them. So, she relayed her morning, including the call from her attorney regarding court.

"Attorneys can be so narrow-minded," Laura said. "They just want you to cover your rear. If you ask me—"

Stacy interjected, "We didn't ask because we already know your stance on the situation. Yes, we agree that Julie and her partner did nothing wrong, so they shouldn't be getting sued."

That summed up her friends' views on the case, but Julie wasn't personally being sued. The medical practice and Dr. Garcia were. She was merely an unfortunate person caught in the middle.

"What are you going to do?" Stacy asked. "It doesn't sound safe for you, even with the bodyguard."

That moment flooded Julie with emotions, recalling the deep despair she had seen in Rodney's eyes as he revealed his helplessness in protecting her. It broke her heart to witness him bear that burden, and she felt an intense urge to reach out, to help him realize it wasn't his fault—that sometimes, life unfolded in ways they couldn't control. But now, she had to reassure her friends that she would be okay, even though she had no idea what her life plan was after leaving the hospital.

"I honestly don't know," she admitted. "We haven't discussed it yet." She was concerned Rodney might send her into hiding at the safe house he mentioned earlier. Not that she didn't want to hide, but with so many people depending on her, she couldn't. They needed to devise a solution that would allow her to help her patients.

"Do the police have any idea who's doing this to you?" Laura asked, sitting at the end of the bed near Julie's feet. So much for her sitting too much.

Julie had no idea. She expected a visit from the police, but since she had been asleep for most of her time in the hospital, they must have come and gone. She was certain Rodney had sent them away, wanting to speak only with the chief of police because of their professional relationship.

She also wondered what had happened to the people who had worked with Rodney and were investigating. No word about their status had reached her—even when she'd eavesdropped. It seemed they were back at square one. This heightened her fear of not knowing whether a colleague, patient—past or present—or stranger was out to hurt her. How was she supposed to function?

"I don't know," Julie finally said, shaking her head. "I haven't heard anything, but I've been out of it since they brought me to the hospital."

"If you ask me—" Laura started, pointing her finger as though she meant to emphasize a point.

"No one did," Stacy interrupted, cutting her off. "Now we just want you to be safe."

Laura nodded. "Yeah, we do." Then she smiled. "Would you share one of those cuties at the door with me?"

It took a moment, but soon, the women burst into giggles. Their laughter was delightful, allowing her to forget how her life had fallen apart momentarily. "Go for it. I'm falling all over them." Then she added, "Just watch out for the one they call 'Pup.' He talks incessantly about dogs."

"I love dogs!" Laura exclaimed, her smile

illuminating the room.

Julie laughed and said, "Yeah. You're not really that crazy about them."

As the three women engaged in light-hearted conversation, Julie felt relief. Despite the burden of her troubles, she found comfort in the presence of friends—an unwavering support system she could always depend on. With Rodney now part of that circle, she needed to dismantle the professional façade that had kept them apart, allowing herself to be vulnerable and authentic. This openness defined what true friendship really meant.

In the wake of Rodney's loss, her need for connection resonated deeply with him, compelling her to become a confidante. She sensed he needed someone to lean on, someone who could help him reclaim the parts of himself that grief had overshadowed. Julie was determined to be that anchor for him, supporting his healing and helping him find redemption.

Now, the question that lingered in her mind: How could she weave their journeys of healing and growth together? That was her dilemma.

Chapter Thirteen

IT TOOK A long time to get Julie released from the hospital. It seemed like every nurse and doctor stopped by to wish her well, and her friends lingered far too long. He had hated leaving her side during their time together, but he understood it was a personal matter among friends. He didn't belong in that category.

He might one day, and perhaps he was heading that way. She didn't pull away when he held her hand. Instead, she placed her hand over his to comfort him.

But could he really protect her? That thought hung over him.

"Hey, Doc," Grits said as he and Boss approached him outside Julie's room while she changed her clothes. He'd offered to help, but she'd quickly declined and shot him a death glare. Oh well, soon enough.

He straightened up from the wall. It couldn't be good with both Alpha and Bravo team leaders coming toward him. "Hey, Boss. Grits." He nodded at them as he spoke their names. "What's up?"

"We need to pull Alpha Team for an op," Boss commanded.

Rodney's heart froze. He was on Alpha team. Was he being reassigned? No, he needed to secure Julie's safety. "Understood," he replied, swallowing the lump in his throat. He attempted to find the right words to stay behind while his team left without him.

Boss firmly gripped his shoulder. "We've decided to keep you in position to continue your mission. Are you okay with that?"

Damn straight, he was good with that.

Now was the right moment to voice his concerns about ensuring Julie's safety. Neither his team leader nor Hamilton had discussed the shooting except to collect information and see if she was all right. No one directly held him responsible for his failure, but he could feel the underlying tension.

"Maybe it would be better if I went with the team and Grits took over." His heart ached as he said that. He didn't want to be separated from Julie while she was in danger, but she deserved the best security, and he wasn't sure he could provide it.

The two team leaders watched him, setting his nerves on edge. What were they assessing? Their gazes locked, and they exchanged a stern nod. Grits turned and left without saying a word. What the hell was happening?

"Time for a chat," Boss ordered.

Doc stayed still. "Julie is getting dressed. She'll be ready to leave soon."

"The men can escort her. We have business to discuss."

This didn't bode well. Doc had never faced a "talk" from his team leader and had a gut feeling he didn't want to now. Doc was keenly aware of his blunder, leaving Julie exposed. He should have secured her at the safe house.

Doc turned to Casper, who was guarding Julie's door. "You've got the team. Get her back to my place and secure it."

Casper nodded, and Doc trailed behind Boss as they walked down the hallway.

"Let's grab some coffee," Boss directed.

Once they took the elevator to the main floor, they quietly went to the cafeteria. After Boss paid for two coffees, they headed to a table in the back corner.

They sipped their coffee before Boss finally said, "Spill it."

Doc feigned ignorance about what the agent meant, but he wasn't naive, and Boss knew it. He had to be honest. Ignoring the truth had previously put women at risk—women whom the men eventually married. He refused to let that happen to Julie.

Cradling the coffee cup in his hand, he cleared his throat. "It's my fault." He held his team leader's gaze. "I should have protected her better."

Boss leaned back and narrowed his eyes. "Are you God?"

Doc furrowed his brow. "Of course not,"

"So, you can't say you would have protected her any better. I heard you acted as soon as the threat was recognized. Unfortunately, they fired a shot before you could get to her."

"I wasn't quick enough," he argued.

Boss sighed heavily. "What's this really about? Is it

Simon or Dr. Banks?"

Hell, he didn't know. He hadn't shielded Simon from danger, and tragically, Simon lost his life. Now, he realized he hadn't provided enough protection for Julie, and the thought of her possibly facing a similar fate sent chills down his spine. "I think I've lost my edge," he murmured in despair, grappling with a gnawing sense of failure and the weight of his responsibilities.

Boss shook his head and waved his hand dismissively, saying, "Nonsense."

As Boss scrutinized him with piercing eyes, Doc felt a tight knot in his stomach, a powerful impulse to squirm under the intensity of his team leader's gaze.

"Would you like to step back on this one?"

His gut clenched at the thought of leaving Julie's protection to someone else. Should he be the Alpha or give her the best option available? Until now, he'd believed that was him, but if his team leader was questioning it…. Doc shrugged. "I don't know." Then he cleared his throat. "I mean, I should, but I don't want to."

"Why not?"

The words felt heavy on his tongue, but he finally released them into the air. "Because I'm going to marry that woman someday."

Boss raised his eyebrows. "Ah, I see."

Doc remembered Boss's unwavering commitment during Sugar's difficulties. He realized that trusting someone else with Julie's destiny was a weight he couldn't endure.

"Do you love her?" Boss asked, his voice a low rumble that echoed softly in the brightly lit room.

Did he? He barely knew her. Yet, deep down in his heart, he felt the undeniable pull that had started that fateful night in the alley. "I believe so."

Boss leaned forward and wrapped his large hands around his coffee cup. "Well, how about this? Let's give Grits control of the team—" He raised a hand to steady Doc when he began to interrupt. "And you'll remain her main bodyguard. That way, the decisions will be made without a muddled mind."

Could he truly give up control over Julie's protection? None of the other men who had married their troubled partners had ever chosen to do so. They had remained resolutely at the forefront of the cases, bravely fighting for the safety and well-being of their loved ones. Doc grimaced at the painful memories that flooded back to him. Most of those situations had only worsened for the women involved.

"I can stay by her side?" Doc asked for clarification.

His team leader nodded slowly, his expression unreadable. "We can do that. However, the decision-making process is outside your control unless an emergency arises. Can you accept that?"

He would need to commit to this path, regardless of its uncertainty. The question whether it was the right choice loomed heavily, and his mind wrestled with the weight of the decision ahead. Whatever course he ultimately chose had to prioritize Julie's well-being. "I can."

"Doc," Boss began, "you haven't lost your edge as an agent. What you've lost is a close friend you haven't mourned yet and an incident that couldn't have been foreseen."

Doc nodded in agreement. He hadn't mourned Simon because Julie's problem immediately claimed his attention. Naturally, he had immersed himself in her world.

"So, when will you tell her she's meant to be your wife?" Boss asked with a sly grin.

He had no clue. It was crucial to help her move past the "patient ethics" dilemma weighing on her. He realized he had chosen to fire her, so couldn't they find a way to connect on a personal level now? Was it possible to pursue a relationship that wouldn't conflict with her ethical standards?

Doc shrugged as the weight of the world rested on his shoulders. "I don't know. How did you tell Sugar?"

"That, my friend, is another story. Sugar and I share a past. You've just met your doctor."

True, but deep down, he desperately needed advice. He had never fallen in love before and didn't want to mess it up. "I'll figure it out," he muttered. Glancing at his watch, a wave of panic washed over him, tightening its grip on his chest. He had been away from Julie for far too long. The thought of her alone at home, without him, sent a jolt of anxiety through him.

Doc stood up, signaling that the meeting was over—regardless of whether he had permission to leave. "I need to go," he said earnestly.

Boss stood up and replied, "How about I give you a ride? It'll be much easier now that the others are gone."

He didn't care if he had to call a ride-share—he needed to get to Julie immediately. He would protect her, no matter who was in charge.

He extended his hand and shook the team leader's. "Thanks, Boss."

Doc felt a heavy weight on his chest, hoping he had made the right choice.

"You've made the right decision." Boss nodded approvingly. "While keeping her company, why not impress her with a glimpse of what a wonderful husband you could be? Captivate her with your charm, sweep her off her feet with your kindness—show her that marrying you could be her best decision yet."

Doc's lips curled into a warm smile. That—he could manage!

Chapter Fourteen

WHEN GRITS MENTIONED that Rodney was meeting with his team leader, Julie became concerned that he might face penalties for her injury. Would they hold him responsible for something beyond his control? She sincerely hoped not. She was ready to advocate for him to ensure his record remained unblemished if they did.

She felt an impossibly heavy burden as she navigated her fear during the drive, particularly on the return trip. Without Rodney by her side, an overwhelming sense of vulnerability washed over her, making her feel like a deer caught in headlights, exposed and defenseless against the looming threat.

Confusion and fear tore through her—a tempest swirling in her chest. It had become painfully clear that she was a madman's target. The uncertainty twisted in her stomach like a knife as she desperately hoped those tasked with uncovering the truth would find answers before it was too late. This was no longer merely a fear but a nightmare clawing into reality.

Could this really be about Carlos or the Newmans? She had always seen the good in everyone, nurturing a belief that neither of them could have harmful intentions. This viewpoint underscored her unwavering optimism and raised questions about the possible naivety of such a perspective. In her mind, the very idea of betrayal by those she trusted seemed unimaginable.

Carlos and his wife, Renee, were her friends. They had always treated her kindly.

Deep in thought, she jumped when her phone rang. Fumbling with her purse using her right hand, she rushed to find her phone and answer it before the caller hung up. Managing tasks one-handed was challenging, and she felt the weight of all her patients who had experienced limited limb movement after surgery.

She found the phone and answered the call. "Hello, Mary," she said to Carlos's office assistant.

"Dr. Banks, you need to come to the clinic. Someone has trashed your office."

Julie sat on the bed's edge in disbelief. "What did you just say?"

"Someone has trashed your office."

Overwhelmed by the surrounding chaos, she struggled to comprehend the magnitude of such wanton destruction. Was someone desperately searching for a patient file, or had the madman pursuing her orchestrated this scene? A wave of despair washed over her, and her shoulders sagged under uncertainty. At that moment, all she wanted was Rodney. The reason eluded her, but the longing surged within her, an ache for his presence that she couldn't ignore.

"Don't touch anything, Mary. Have you called the police?" Maybe Chief Wise had some answers for her.

"No. Should I?"

She should, but Julie wouldn't let them poke around in patient files. She had to follow HIPAA regulations. "Wait until I'm there. I'm on my way." She ended the call.

Now, how was she supposed to persuade these men to take her to a scene that only contributed to the disarray of her life?

When she heard the door open and close, her heart fluttered excitedly. She listened intently, and then her heart leaped for joy. Rodney was back. Just the thought of him sent butterflies dancing in her stomach. He would take her to her office because he understood her need to control something in her life.

What she couldn't control was how she felt about Rodney, which concerned her. Yes, she had come to rely on him for her safety, but she also enjoyed his company —more than she should, considering their doctor-patient relationship.

Driven by a profound sense of anticipation, she flung open the bedroom door and rushed to the stairwell to meet him. A bright smile lit up her face as she descended the stairs, but her heart sank at the sight of him. He seemed to have been at a disadvantage in his meeting with the team leader, serving as a stark reminder of his struggles. Surely, he needed her support now more than ever, and she wouldn't let this moment slip by without offering him the encouragement he so desperately needed.

When he caught her eye, their gazes locked, and everyone in the room must have felt the heat flaring between them. Someone cleared their throat, and she knew it had not gone unnoticed.

She broke eye contact and fiddled with her sling, sending a sharp pain through her arm.

"What's up, Julie?" Rodney asked as he approached her. "You look like something's bothering you."

She did—him. However, it felt like the worst time to let her heart wander. Her life was filled with danger and turmoil, demanding that she maintain a careful distance. Yet, despite the upheaval, her heart had other plans, whispering for closeness she couldn't resist.

"My office—" she started, then cleared her throat and looked back at Rodney. "Someone has trashed my office at the clinic."

Rodney narrowed his eyes. "How do you know this?"

"The clinic assistant called and let me know."

"Was the clinic completely wrecked or just your office?" Rodney asked. He glanced at Casper and Pup as the men exited the front door.

She hadn't thought to ask. She assumed it was only hers since Mary referred to her office. However, they could have destroyed the entire clinic. "I'm not sure."

He crossed his arms over his broad chest. The muscles in his arms bulged, catching her attention. "I'm guessing you want to see for yourself."

"Um," she said, licking her lips. As she mentally shook her head to clear it, she continued, "I mean, yes. I have to. The police can't be there without me because of my patient records."

Rodney wore a knowing smile that made her cheeks redden. "Then let's check it out. The guys are already getting a vehicle ready."

That's why they left. She thought it was to give them privacy. "I just need to grab my purse from upstairs."

He nodded. "You handle that while I make a call."

Julie hurried up the stairs to grab her purse and phone. When she returned downstairs, she heard Rodney say, "Thanks, Chief."

Shocked, Julie gasped. "Did you call the chief of police about my office? That's a minor issue compared to what he handles daily."

Rodney pocketed his phone and extended his hand, a gesture that appeared simple yet filled with unspoken reassurance. She grasped his hand, stepping into the outside world, where vehicles waited silently. The warmth of his grip enveloped her in a cocoon of safety, shielding her from her thoughts. His presence was profoundly soothing, radiating an innate calmness that whispered promises of comfort. In that moment, she sensed he had the strength to confront her demons and face the shadows within her world.

She felt lost in both mind and spirit when she let go of Rodney's hand to get into the SUV. She needed to ponder the ethics concerning a former patient—one who had released her from his care. Perhaps there was a loophole for such a situation.

Despite the lingering doubt gnawing at her heart, she couldn't shake the unsettling feeling. The burden of strict ethical standards loomed over her, casting a shadow over every thought of Rodney and what they could become.

"Earth to Julie!" Rodney called, snapping her out of her heavy thoughts.

She gazed at him, puzzled. "What's going on?"

"I've been calling your name for ages. Where have you been?"

Julie shrugged. Her attempt at a smile faltered. "Oh, you know, just lost in thought—about everything, honestly."

Rodney sighed. "Do you want to share what's on your mind?"

She did, but what should she share? The fact that someone is trying to kill her? The possibility that she might be falling for a patient—no, a former patient? Or that her life has been turned upside down? It all felt too heavy for a conversation in the SUV with others listening, so she chose to discuss what they had in common.

"Does HIS have any information about who might be trying to harm me?"

Rodney shook his head. "We have eliminated the Newmans."

He didn't elaborate, but she understood his meaning. They hadn't removed her clinic partner. "Oh," was all she could say. Was Carlos trying to harm her? Why? She hadn't expected her testimony in his case to attract this level of attention. Was it about the practice? Did he want to take it over without compensating her? In their wills, they had both stated that their share of the practice would go to the other partner in the event of their death.

Could that be it? He'd rather pay hired killers to take her out than buy her out? It seemed so sterile.

"Of course," Doc said, considering whether Carlos was her madman. "With the shooting, that eliminates the hospital, so we're certain you're the target."

She figured that out on her own. But why trash her office? That wouldn't harm her personally. It might hurt her a bit professionally, though, if files go missing. It didn't seem to make sense.

Julie closed her eyes, prepared to abandon all the danger that had come to define her life. At least Rodney and the others had stuck around. Naturally, she intended to compensate them for their time and expenses, regardless of the cost.

Grits, seated in the front passenger seat, began outlining their entry and maneuver steps. Julie turned her gaze towards Rodney, noticing the tension in his jaw—a subtle yet telling sign. Had they truly usurped his command? Was this the very scenario his team leader had encountered? If that was indeed the case, relief washed over her that they had entrusted Rodney's care to her.

Grits might expect her to go to the safe house instead of Rodney's, a prospect she weighed carefully. There was something undeniably appealing about the warm charm of Rodney's home. It may not have been the expansive estate she grew up on, but it radiated a sense of belonging that resonated deeply within her.

As they stopped before the clinic, Julie waited while the agents inspected the small building. She and Carlos saw only a few patients each week—those they had treated in the ER who needed follow-up care. It wasn't a major money-maker, so surely Carlos wouldn't want to kill her over it.

Rodney nodded and glanced at her. "Are you ready?"

Was she? She couldn't endure another hit to her life,

but it had happened, and she had to confront it. Putting on a bravado she didn't truly feel, she smiled. "Yes."

Walking into the clinic, Julie appreciated having Rodney right beside her. Earlier, he had been a step ahead, like a bodyguard. Now, he walked as her equal. Perhaps that was the change his team leader had anticipated. She wanted to know, but their relationship hadn't progressed to that level of personal understanding.

Mary stood at her desk, grimacing. "Dr. Banks, I'll help you clean your office and organize the files."

Julie smiled and nodded. "Thank you, Mary." She paused outside the closed door of her office and took a deep breath. Why had the agent who cleared this area shut the door again? It must be worse than she anticipated, and they wanted to give her time to prepare.

She closed her eyes and silently counted to ten. Afterward, she opened them and exhaled. Extending her right hand, she opened the office door.

The next thing she knew, she was in Rodney's arms, crying.

Chapter Fifteen

DOC FELT HELPLESS. He had helped Julie with any overturned furniture, but he couldn't assist her with the disorganized files. All he could do was stand by while her heart broke for each destroyed file. It took her and Mary three days to rearrange them and confirm they were all accounted for. Ultimately, Julie removed her sling to work faster. He knew it must have hurt, but she pushed through the pain.

It also took them that long to discover that the assistant she had fired—Mary's twin, Gary—was the vandal.

HIS hadn't moved in on him yet as the team investigated to see if he could also be the one attempting to end Julie's life. So far, that didn't seem to be the case. The vandalism suggested pettiness and inexperience, while the bomb and shooting represented an entirely different level of evil.

Doc was ready to hang him from the yardarm. The kid had made Julie cry. She landed in his arms, and he offered her comfort—until she realized what she had done by turning to him. The kiss he placed on her head might have been too much for this stage of their relationship.

Since then, she had become withdrawn, choosing to eat in her room instead of with him and the other men. He didn't like this change. She was distancing herself, and he wanted to help her, but he didn't know how.

That evening, Doc decided to act. He wouldn't force her to join the men for dinner but instead try to dine with her. So, he brought his meal to her room and knocked, hoping she wouldn't turn him away. It was time for them to grow closer. He wouldn't let her pull away.

When the door opened, Doc's breath caught. She had changed into pajama pants and a top that accentuated her curves better than the jeans and sweater she wore that morning.

"Rodney," she murmured.

He raised his plate and drink. "I thought I'd join you tonight. We have a lot to talk about."

Her eyebrows arched into a V, and she asked, "We do?"

Rodney nodded, pushed past her, and said, "We do."

When Julie didn't challenge him, he smiled and placed his plate of food on the small desk next to her dinner. He turned to her. "First of all," he said as he reached for her, pulling her into his arms. "I'm going to kiss you like I've wanted to since the moment we met. If you don't want this, you'd better speak up now."

When Julie fell silent, he lowered his head and gently nibbled her lower lip. He smiled inwardly when she gasped for breath. "Your lips are so soft," he murmured against them as he captured her mouth in a kiss. His lips moved over hers, and he knew he had won when she wrapped her arms around his neck. "Julie," he whispered, pulling her tightly against him, his arousal twitching.

When Julie moaned, he thrust his tongue inside her mouth, stroking gently until her tongue joined in the dance of lovers. Their tongues swirled around each other —teasing and taunting the other.

Doc ran his fingers through her hair, tilting her head slightly to kiss her more deeply. Her flavor intoxicated him. Yes, she had a hint of their dinner, but her sweetness was irresistible, and he loved it.

As his dick decided to move and show her how he felt, and she didn't push back, he ran his hands down her back to her butt and pulled her against him. She had to know this was more than a make-out session. He wouldn't take her if she didn't want it, but he was ready. He hoped she was also.

"Julie, you taste amazing," he murmured against her lips.

"Hmm," she said, her eyes closed and a blissful look on her face.

"Look at me, baby." He waited until she opened her eyes, savoring the desire reflected in them. She wanted him, and she couldn't deny it. "I want you."

A different kind of fire ignited within her.

She jumped back in shock. "I—I can't do this."

Doc squinted. "Why not?"

"You know why."

"That's bullshit. I'm no longer your patient. It's simply an excuse."

She ran her fingers over her swollen lips. "I—"

Doc shook his head. He wouldn't give up on this woman, but now wasn't the time to push. "Okay." He cleared his throat and adjusted himself, allowing her to see what she'd done to him. He didn't want the men to see that, though. "I understand you're returning to the hospital in the morning."

Julie nodded. "Yes, I'll follow up on Dr. Sanders's patients while he takes his wife to visit her dying mother."

Nodding, Doc walked to the door. "I'll see you then." He stepped outside and took deep breaths to calm himself. It wasn't until he was almost down the stairs that he remembered he had left his dinner in her room.

Grits was finishing a call when he came back to the main floor.

"I've got some news," the agent said. "Devon discovered significant transfers in Dr. Garcia's bank accounts that align with the bombing and shooting. However," he raised his hand to keep the agents from getting too excited. "He also has other substantial withdrawals that are similar in nature. Jesse and Brad are going to speak with him."

Doc was eager to confront that bastard. Dr. Garcia walked in on Julie cleaning her office and offered no help. That had riled Doc, HIPAA or not.

But he wouldn't abandon Julie now. He would leave the preliminary questioning to his bosses but would see things through to the end once they found the culprits.

"Also," Grits said with a smile, "they found the SUV that held the shooter. It belongs to a lowlife who claims to know nothing. Chief Wise is giving us some leeway with him, so I'm sure we'll uncover who the shooter was and who hired him."

Progress. Doc couldn't be more satisfied, especially after the disappointment upstairs. He hadn't expected to make love to her tonight, but he had looked forward to spending more time with her and getting to know her better.

He wanted to run up and tell Julie everything, but figured she wouldn't answer the door. He'd save it until morning. Or should he hold back on Dr. Garcia? He didn't want her to ruin any chance he had to change his course, and they wouldn't be able to catch him. He'd think about that after a good night's sleep.

After Grits, Pup, and Doc talked about the recent developments, Grits departed, leaving Pup on duty with Casey while Doc tossed and turned in his bed, wishing he were across the hall in Julie's room.

The next day arrived far too quickly, and Doc was irritable from lack of sleep. When Grits met him downstairs with coffee and a smile, remarking that he looked like shit, Doc felt like punching him. "Get out," he muttered.

"No can do. We have a busy day, and Dr. Garcia is in today."

That caught Doc's attention and made him turn his head. Why were they letting that madman work alongside Julie?

"Relax, Doc. I can see your wheels turning," Grits said.

The front door swung open as Cowboy strolled in, his face all bright smiles. "Boy howdy, you look like shit,

Doc."

Doc responded by flipping him off.

Pup and Casey slipped out the door, the kid yawning as if he had never slept a day.

"Why on earth is everyone so cheerful?" Doc asked as he poured himself a cup of coffee. "She's going to be working next to a man who might want her dead."

"Because we'll be there to catch every move he makes," Cowboy said, opening the refrigerator. "Whose turn is it to get breakfast?"

"Yours," said Doc.

"Ah, hell. I had to deal with that tooth fairy situation last night, and this morning was chaos at home." Cowboy pulled his phone from his pants pocket. "Hang on."

He walked away.

Doc looked at Grits. "So, tell me why?"

"First, we're not sure if it's Dr. Garcia. Second, if it is, this is the perfect time to watch his activities and protect your woman from him."

"She's not my woman," Doc grumbled. He wanted her to be his but would scream if she didn't get past this patient ethics thing.

"Keep telling yourself that."

"What does he keep telling himself?" Julie asked as she walked down the stairs in blue scrubs that highlighted the vibrant blue of her eyes.

"Nothing," Doc replied tersely. "Want some coffee?"

"Yes, please." Julie tossed her purse over her shoulder and walked up to him, accepting the cup he had poured.

Cowboy reappeared, smiling at Julie. "Good morning, Dr. Banks." Then he turned to Doc. "Ballpark is bringing us something."

Grits snorted. "You're lucky you didn't arrive last."

The rest of the morning flew by in a blur. Doc found himself more focused on Dr. Garcia than on Julie. He didn't trust the man, fearing he might have bribed someone to hurt her. How long would it take to trace where the payments went? Devon was supposed to be the best there was.

Julie hadn't received approval to perform surgery, but she spent the day checking in on Dr. Sanders's surgical patients. She exhibited a fantastic bedside manner that put every patient at ease—sometimes perhaps a little too much.

Mr. Watkins, a high school history teacher in Room 405, spent half an hour lecturing him about World War I, during which Rodney found himself yawning. However, she smiled and took her time with him. When he asked her why she devoted so much time to this patient, she explained that some of her patients were lonely.

"Some patients have no visitors or calls to check on their well-being. He's alone, and I have the time."

Doc's pride in her grew with every patient they saw. Of course, he didn't care for the trailing students since he had to play second fiddle, but he remained by her side in the rooms.

She was an exceptional professor. He wondered why she only took on the supervisory role at the hospital and didn't teach classes. Still, he recognized that she dedicated extra time to patients instead of seeking additional income.

After Julie dismissed her students, she gathered her belongings from the doctor's locker room and followed the agents toward the exit. Rodney stayed by her side, ready in case Dr. Garcia attempted something at the last minute.

As the overhead speaker blared, "Code Blue. Room 405. Code Blue. Room 405," Doc felt a surge of urgency. He followed closely behind Julie as she rushed to the stairwell, yanked the door open, and climbed the stairs two at a time.

Chapter Sixteen

WHEN THEY ENTERED the room, a group of medical professionals attended to Mr. Watkins. Julie stepped in and allowed the doctor to take the lead. It was the first time Doc had seen her follow, and she excelled at not trying to take control during a crisis.

Doc believed she was eager to act and would do so if the doctor made a mistake. That must be why they considered her for chief of surgery—she could lead while knowing when to follow and offer advice. He hoped she would secure the position when it opened next month, as the current chief was retiring.

"He's stable," she said with weary eyes and concern.

"What the hell happened?" Dr. Boyd, the doctor in charge, asked. "This man was in recovery and doing well."

Just when Julie appeared ready to intervene and end the man's tirade, a nurse stated, "I just administered the medication Dr. Banks prescribed."

Dr. Boyd approached the pharmacy's rolling cart. After several keystrokes, he turned to Julie and said, "Everyone leave the room."

Doc hoped the man wasn't referring to him since he wasn't leaving her alone, particularly with someone who looked ready to blow his top.

After everyone left, Dr. Boyd remarked, "His record clearly indicates that he's allergic to oxycodone. Why did you prescribe it?"

Julie appeared surprised. "I didn't prescribe it."

"The computer says you did," he insisted. "You know I have to report this."

Doc watched as Julie's posture stiffened and straightened. "I did not prescribe oxycodone for this patient. I prescribed hydromorphone because of his allergy."

"You'd better get your story straight because the computer doesn't lie."

Julie narrowed her eyes. "Are you implying that I'm lying?"

"What I'm saying," Dr. Boyd clarified, "is that there's a contradiction. Since this patient coded, I need to report the discrepancy."

"I understand," Julie finally said.

Doc watched her stand tall and strong against the accusation aimed at her. He wondered what would happen next. Come to think of it, he remembered her mentioning what she had prescribed when he was there. "Dr. Boyd," he began.

"And who the hell are you? You look like some militant guy in all black with a weapon at your side. And the men at the door—what the hell is going on?"

"That's beside the point," Doc said. "I heard Ju—Dr. Banks as she entered the medication selection. She acknowledged his aversion to oxycodone and chose another option."

"Well, what she said and what she entered into the computer are two different things. The pharmacy relies on what is entered in the system."

Doc didn't like this guy, but he made a valid point. He couldn't imagine Julie making such a grave mistake.

"I have other patients to see," Dr. Boyd said as he left the room, leaving behind the medical cart used to save Mr. Watkins.

Julie turned to the patient and checked his pulse at his wrist. She gently placed it back on the bed and sighed heavily. "I need to see my boss," she said to him as she slowly walked toward the door.

"What happens next?" Doc asked.

She shrugged. "Now, I'm going to see my boss."

That didn't seem fair. She hadn't done anything wrong. The pharmacy must've made a mistake.

They left, and when Doc couldn't follow her into her boss's office, he realized this situation was more serious than Julie had implied. Otherwise, she wouldn't have cared if he heard the facts since he had witnessed them. Could he offer another perspective on what occurred? Now that he thought about it, the students were also with her when she clearly stated that the man was allergic to that specific opioid.

But Doc had to allow her to manage her business. He didn't know enough about the medical field to discuss the current administrative procedures.

Julie appeared defeated as she left the office. "I'm ready to go."

Doc nodded and placed his hand on her back, guiding her to stand beside him and between the other agents. They hadn't encountered any issues with Dr. Garcia today. In fact, he had been especially attentive to her.

Once they got into the vehicle, Doc turned to her. "Do you want to talk about it?"

He could see the tears welling up in her eyes, and he wanted to reach over and wipe them away.

"I'm on leave, waiting for a medical review board at the hospital." Her voice was strong, but her body language indicated that she worried or disagreed. He leaned toward the latter because he didn't think she would worry about something she had done correctly.

"How long will that take?" he asked, longing to pull her into his arms and comfort her.

"It'll only be a few days since the hospital has been short-staffed with surgeons." She turned and looked out her window, ending his interrogation.

Doc listened through his earpiece as Cowboy declared that the house was clear. They drove the SUVs to the door and hurried Julie inside. He wasn't taking any more chances with her life.

The one positive outcome of today was that she was put on leave, allowing them to spend time together. He then recalled that court had been rescheduled and they would need to attend when summoned.

"When will you be getting your stitches out?" Doc asked her.

Julie glanced at her arm. "I'll take them out."

He hadn't considered that option, but being a

medical professional must be a benefit.

Later, Julie had dinner with the agents, and Doc resented sharing her. He suspected she had come down to eat to avoid a repeat of the previous night. Little did she know there would be many more repeats. In fact, they were just getting started.

After clearing the dishes, Grits headed out for the evening, leaving Pup and Casey as the indoor protectors and Cowboy and Nemo outside. He enjoyed this role because it gave him time to spend with Julie.

"Can I talk to you, Julie?" Doc asked before she could go up the stairs.

She nodded and walked over to him.

With Pup in the living room, Doc didn't want any witnesses. "Out on the back patio."

Doc took pride in his small patio. Although well-landscaped, it included a hot tub he would love to enjoy with Julie.

A nearly full moon lit up the otherwise dark area. He cleared his throat after they settled into their stools at a high-top table. "I want to talk about last night."

Julie nodded. "I figured you might." She crossed her arms over her chest, effectively closing herself off.

"First, I'm not sorry. I like you, Julie. I want to get to know you better."

"I—"

"I understand your concerns about ethics, but you shouldn't worry."

She snorted. "That's just what I need—another review board."

Okay, this wasn't going well. He had just told the

woman that he liked her, but she didn't respond in kind. He knew she wanted him. No woman would kiss like that if she didn't at least like the man. At least, no woman he'd commit to.

"Julie," he said, reaching across the table to take her hand from her chest. He held it gently with his own. "Do you want me?"

Their gazes locked in a blaze of desire and heat. She couldn't deny what she wanted. He would know.

"It doesn't matter," she said.

He looked around for inspiration. How could he reach her? Suddenly, an idea struck him. He met her gaze once more with renewed intensity. "Isn't there some kind of moonlight exception to this rule?"

When she didn't respond immediately, he felt anxious. Then she smiled widely. "There just might be."

With a broad grin, he tugged at her hand. "Then come here."

Without breaking eye contact, Julie slowly stood and positioned herself between his legs. With the high chairs, they were at eye level, face to face.

Doc wrapped his arms around her waist, and she placed hers around his neck.

"I'm tired of fighting my feelings for you, Rodney. I don't know where our relationship might go, but I want you."

That was all he needed. He kissed her fiercely, indifferent to the possibility of bruising their lips. He needed to taste her…to touch her…to have her. This time, they wouldn't stop except to make their way upstairs.

Doc pulled her closer, spreading his legs to

accommodate her entirely. Sitting as he was, his dick was aching, not just with desire for her, but because he needed to adjust himself. Breaking the hungry kiss, he took several deep breaths, then shifted in the seat.

"Julie," he whispered against her lips.

"Rodney," she murmured.

He ran his fingers through her hair, gently adjusting the angle of her head. Anticipation surged within him, strengthening his resolve to be with her tonight as he trailed kisses down her soft neck. Her pulse raced, and he knew she was just as aroused as he was.

"Inside," he said in a gruff voice.

She paused. "What about Pup?"

"What about him?" Doc didn't intend to invite the kid into the bedroom with them.

"He'll know what we're up to," she said shyly.

What were they, teenagers sneaking around behind their parents' backs? Doc pressed his forehead to hers, their noses nearly touching. "Honey, with the heat between us, they probably already think we are."

Even in the moonlight, he could see her charming blush.

"So, are we going upstairs, or am I just going to get you undressed out here?"

Julie chuckled. "Your place or mine?"

"That's my line," he said with a playful grin, taking her hand and guiding her into his home.

Chapter Seventeen

WHEN THEY SNEAKED through the back door, Pup and Casey ignored them. Or, at least, Julie hoped they were ignoring them and not just pretending. Somehow, though, she doubted that anything went unnoticed by the agent and his pup.

Butterflies fluttered in her stomach as they entered his room and quietly locked the door behind them. She was going to do this. Julie didn't care whether he was a patient or not. She wanted him with every fiber of her being and wasn't planning to hold back.

She tingled under his intense gaze as if his hands followed his eyes, touching and caressing every inch of her clothed body.

As if she were a fragile doll, Rodney removed her sweater slowly. When he pulled it over her head, she saw him looking at her bra-covered breasts. Why hadn't she worn something sexier? *Because I planned to have sex with him tonight.* She knew it would eventually happen because her resolve had been slipping, but she hadn't planned that night.

Reaching around her body, he unclasped and slipped

her bra from her shoulders, exposing her breasts.

Rodney moved closer and rested his forehead against hers. "God, you're beautiful." He reached up and rubbed his thumb over her taut nipple, making her catch her breath. "I can't wait to explore every inch of your sexy body." He raised his eyebrows in a sultry manner. "From the top of your head to the tips of your toes."

Julie reached out and wrapped her hand around the prominent bulge in his black cargo pants. "No. I'll explore, especially here." She squeezed him and was rewarded with a deep groan.

Breaking their connection, she lifted his black long-sleeved T-shirt with HIS logo over his head. Her gaze wandered over his chest, noting the nipple piercings, and her heart raced.

"I think it's time we get rid of the rest of our clothes." His deep, gravelly voice brought a smile to her face.

She reached down and slid her jeans off, then her panties, again wishing she'd worn something sexy instead of practical. When he stood after removing his garments, her breath caught at the size of him. Trembling with need, she reached out to his chest to feel his taut muscles.

Rodney remained still as she explored his chest, his nipple piercing, and the healed wounds she found. She knew each had its story, but now wasn't the time for them—maybe between sessions.

Her face flushed at the thought of several sessions with this large man. Sure, she'd fantasized about it, but now it was reality. She didn't want to mess it up and say something stupid like *"patie—."*

As she explored his chest, shoulders, and arms, Rodney groaned but showed remarkable restraint by remaining still and refraining from grabbing her and tossing her onto the bed to assert control. Of course, she wouldn't stop him if he did.

Gazing into his passionate eyes, warmth surged through her, and she smiled. "You're perfect."

"My turn?" he asked, raising his brows.

Julie smiled enticingly. "I'm not finished."

He laughed softly. "Oh, absolutely you are, or else we'll rush through everything because I can't last much longer." He grasped her waist, making her giggle as he walked her backward until the backs of her knees brushed against the bed.

"I've been waiting a long time to have you in my bed. I've dreamed about it every night."

She wasn't ready to tell him that she'd pleasured herself at the thought of them together. Not yet, anyway. "Oh, yeah?" she teased as her hand slid down his chest to his cock. Encircling him, he let out a deep, guttural groan. She loved the effect she had on him.

"You're killing me," he said, pulling her hand back. "I go first."

Before she could voice an objection, he pulled her close, capturing her mouth and devouring her lips with a ferocity she hadn't expected—but loved.

As his mouth moved over hers, he gently lowered her onto the bed, her knees bent over the edge. She reached down to push herself up, but he stopped her.

"Nope. I want to explore and taste you first."

With a playful smile, she let her hands drop and

opened her arms wide. She was more than okay with it because she craved it with every fiber of her being. "Go on, then."

Rodney stood over her, raking his gaze across her body, igniting a deep-seated hunger within her. She had never desired a man as much as she wanted to be with him. Yet, it wasn't solely physical. She cherished his company. Her heart swelled with emotion during the days they spent with their heads close together at the hospital while she shared her concerns about her students or patients. Could it be love? She certainly hoped so, considering she was taking this leap at the risk of her career.

No, she wouldn't think about that now. They were taking advantage of that moonlight exception. She'd handle any consequences as they came. Rodney was worth whatever a review board could throw at her.

"Where did you go?" he asked, his brows drawn together in a V.

Julie smiled and shook her head. "Nowhere." She squirmed. "I thought you were going to explore."

He smiled widely. "Oh, I am."

"Then stop talking and just do it before I flip you over and figure it out myself."

He stood up straight between her legs. "You wouldn't," he challenged.

She could easily lock her legs around his and flip them in bed, but that wasn't what she wanted. No, she did want that, but she wanted him to be in charge the first time. There would be plenty of other opportunities for her to take charge.

Woah. That meant more than just this exception, and she was okay with that, too.

Rodney leaned closer to her lips. "I thought so," he said before capturing them in a kiss so intense that she whimpered with pleasure.

His hand slid to her breast, moving over it, playing with it until it ached with the desire that inhabited the rest of her body. Breaking the kiss, he slid his lips down her neck to her breast, pulling the taut nipple into his mouth. While his mouth worked her right breast, his hand explored her left one, teasing it.

Her head sank into the pillow as her hands roamed through his short hair. The blend of softness and stubble from his closely cropped beard wreaked havoc on her body—a sensation she wouldn't trade for anything.

As Rodney's hand slipped down between her legs, she moaned in pleasure and anticipation of him tasting her, lapping his tongue around her, driving her over the edge.

Julie gasped at the abrupt pounding on the door.

"Doc," Pup said, "sorry to interrupt, but there's a phone call for you."

Rodney rested his head against her chest and groaned. "Tell them I'm busy."

"I don't think you want to do that."

Footsteps faded as Pup descended the stairs.

Rodney looked up at her with pleading eyes. "Please wait for me. I'll be right back."

Once again, feeling embarrassed by the men in the house, Julie shook her head. "No, I'll go back to my room."

"Julie—" he murmured.

"Come to me when you're finished."

With a stern gaze, he smiled. "Don't lock me out. I know exactly where the key is." He winked, got to his feet, and dressed in what had to be record time.

After he left the room, Julie dressed, 86ing her underclothes since she wouldn't have anything on when he returned.

Then, it dawned on her. Someone might be bringing news about her. She nibbled her lower lip. Should she eavesdrop again or rely on Rodney to tell her what happened?

She jumped when her phone rang. Who could be calling this late in the evening? Glancing at the clock, she realized it wasn't even eight o'clock. *Wow.*

She glanced at her screen and answered the call. "Hey, Laura."

The background music made it nearly impossible for her to hear. "It's Laura and Stacy. We're out and want you to join us."

She sighed, reflecting on all the nights they had enjoyed drinks after work to unwind and sometimes meet a man. Not Laura, though. She had some secret man she talked about. She and Stacy believed it wasn't true, but who cared as long as her friend was happy?

"You know I can't do that."

"Bring the hunky guys with you," Stacy said. "Laura's even on the lookout tonight."

Surprised, Julie inquired, "Laura?"

"Just a lover's quarrel. But I'm ready for something different tonight. Bring those guys and come on out."

Julie knew the men wouldn't let her go to a bar at that hour when it would be crowded, and they couldn't maintain control. Besides, she had her review board hearing in the morning. She hadn't expected it to come up so soon but had received the message before dinner. She hadn't told Rodney yet and thought it was best to inform him before he made other plans for them.

"I have my review board hearing tomorrow morning," she informed them.

"What?" Stacy asked. "Already?"

Yeah, that's what Julie thought. They convened too quickly. She only hoped they wouldn't decide just as quickly unless it was in her favor. She couldn't imagine how it could be otherwise because she hadn't made a mistake on that order.

"How about we come to see you?" Stacy asked, and Laura chimed in.

She hoped they could, so she would ask Rodney if she could tell her friends where she was staying so they could visit her. They weren't a threat to her.

"You know you can't." She sighed. "But I'll ask. Now, have fun tonight. I'll see you at the hospital tomorrow."

After hanging up the phone, she set it down and stood to get dressed completely—including her undergarments. Once she was presentable, she went to the stairwell and heard, "Devon found what you were looking for."

Rodney said, "Let him know I'm on my way."

Her heart sank when he encountered her in the stairwell.

"I need to step out for a little while," he said, his voice filled with pain. "It shouldn't be long."

Wounded by his decision to leave and his failure to share the reasons, it was more than she could bear. She shrugged. "It's fine. I need my sleep. My review board is at eight o'clock tomorrow morning."

Rodney raised his eyebrows. "When were you going to tell me this?"

Julie headed back upstairs, not wanting him to see her pain. "I just did."

Chapter Eighteen

RODNEY NEVER CAME to her bed that evening. When Julie woke, she was beyond angry with him for toying with her as he had. Was she just a convenience he could play with when she agreed? And to think, she had almost forsaken her patient ethics for him. In fact, she had already done that, but it could have been much worse.

The next day, as she dressed, it pained her not to wear scrubs, but she understood the importance of donning a nice suit for the review board. Although the board wouldn't object to scrubs, a more professional appearance would elicit a positive response to her.

Just as she finished pinning her hair into a bun at the nape of her neck, a knock came at her door. She usually wore a ponytail, but she had always been told it made her look years younger. While that compliment flattered her most of the time, she needed to be serious today. She was risking her chance at becoming chief of surgery and her ability to practice medicine.

"Yes?" she said before answering.

"Julie," Rodney said, "we need to talk."

Oh no, they didn't. The last time they "talked," she

had nearly slept with him. She flung the door open and breezed past him. "No, we don't. Let's go. I don't want to be late."

The drive to the hospital was brutal. They sandwiched her between Rodney and Casper—two rather large men—in the backseat. She guessed they didn't want another occurrence of the shooting.

Tension filled the SUV cabin as Julie focused solely on what she would say to the hospital administrators at her hearing. She had done absolutely nothing wrong, but the order had been erroneous. Had she overlooked it? Had she made a mistake?

No. She always double-checked her medication entries when someone had an allergy. She was sure she didn't include oxycodone for the patient.

"Julie?" Rodney asked.

"Huh?" She glanced at him. "Did you say something?"

"Yes, I need to talk to you."

Not this again. She wouldn't have the conversation about why he stood her up, especially not in front of the other agents. "Later," she said, trying to figure out how she could avoid the conversation then. Right now, she had to be entirely focused.

"Julie—" he pleaded.

"Not right now, Rodney," she said, exasperated. "I need to get ready for this meeting."

He nodded and turned his head toward the window. "I won't be there when the meeting starts," he added, almost as an afterthought.

She turned her head toward him. "What?" That

shouldn't have upset her, but it did. She was a whirlwind of contradictions when it came to this man. One minute, she wanted him with her; the next, she didn't want to see him. One minute, she wanted him; the next, she—well, she still wanted him. Still….

They drove to the front of the hospital, an entrance she seldom utilized since she primarily worked in the emergency room and surgical suites.

Nerves overwhelmed her. Would they fire her for what they deemed to be her fault? She couldn't bear the thought of not working at this hospital. She loved it— and the patients. Even the other doctors that had a god complex.

Casper exited the vehicle, and she followed him. The SUV drove away after he closed the door. What about her protection? While she expected to be safe at the hospital, lately, she didn't feel safe anywhere except at Rodney's home.

The two agents in the second SUV, Cowboy, Pup, and Casey, met them at the front door, and the group walked through the automatic doors.

Julie started to tremble as they made their way to the administrative wing. Even though she had never faced a review board hearing, she had heard they could be brutal.

Casper leaned down to her. "It's okay, Dr. Banks. You're a strong doctor. Just let me know, and remind them you didn't make that error."

She appreciated the brief pep talk but wished it had come from Rodney instead of another agent. Still, it helped calm her nerves. "Thank you, Casper."

Calling these men by nicknames felt strange, yet

they wouldn't share their real names as if they were ashamed of them. Well, she hoped that soon she'd be free of them all and could return to her life.

That had her thinking about Carlos again. Was he behind everything that had been happening to her? Could he have altered the order in the system? She hadn't shared her passcode, but that didn't mean he didn't have it.

It wasn't as if she could accuse him without evidence. Otherwise, her career would be at risk. She would simply have to endure whatever storm the hospital sent her way.

As she approached the conference room, her steps felt heavy, and she struggled to keep pace with the agents. They must have noticed and adjusted their speed to match hers. As much as she hated having these men around her every moment of the day, she would miss the courtesy and protectiveness they offered her.

"Please have a seat, Dr. Banks," the hospital administrator's assistant said. "They'll be with you shortly."

In hospital terminology, "shortly" could mean anything, and she knew this. She sat, attempting not to fidget with her skirt, which might betray her nervousness.

When Casper stood close by, it only heightened her anxiety.

"Can't you at least sit down?"

He smiled and nodded after looking at her for what felt like an eternity. "Sure thing, Doc."

That brought Rodney to her mind as if he had never left. She wished it were him sitting next to her, holding her hand. She abruptly halted that train of thought.

"You know," Casper said, "you've got this. We have no doubts."

The use of "we" made her heart melt. These men were becoming friends with her—friends who would take a bullet for her, which troubled her endlessly—but friends, nonetheless. "Thank you, Casper."

He leaned in closer. "You may call me Ash."

Julie smiled and eased back into her chair. "Thank you, Ash."

"Dr. Banks," the assistant said, "they're ready for you."

So much for relaxation. It flew out the window as soon as she stood. With her shoulders back, she took a deep breath and released it before opening the door.

It was worse than she expected. The five administrators, including her boss, sat on one side of the table, leaving a solitary chair on the other side for her. They scrutinized her as she approached. Unsure if she could sit without permission, she knew better than to upset them right away. "May I sit?"

"Of course." Mr. Baker, the head administrator of the hospital, nodded toward the chair.

Sitting nearly at attention, she left her ankles uncrossed beneath the table, prepared to bolt if necessary.

Mr. Baker cleared his throat. "Dr. Banks, do you know why we're meeting today?"

She wanted to give him a "Duh," like the younger students did with questions like that, but instead, she nodded. "I do."

"Well, indulge me as I summarize." Mr. Baker glanced at the file before him and recounted the details of

Mr. Watkins's near-death experience.

She wanted to scream. Those weren't the facts. She hadn't messed up. It had to be Carlos, but how could she prove it when she was only given a day before the hearing?

After completing the summation, he glanced at each board member. "Does anyone have anything to add?"

Julie hoped not, as that had been more than enough lies. She wanted to scream from her chair that they had it all wrong, but she knew that wouldn't help her situation.

When no one spoke up, she sighed in relief. She didn't want to be caught off guard by anything else.

"I'm going to read the timeline we have of Mr. Watkins's file from your visit until his cardiac arrest." Mr. Baker looked at her questioningly, as if she might object.

She nodded, as though her approval was the key to moving forward.

As the administrator noted the facts as they saw them, Julie quietly reviewed her defense once again. It would be her word against what was on the computer, and they had learned from the beginning that the computer didn't lie.

"Now," Mr. Baker interrupted her preparation. "What do you have to say, Dr. Banks?"

Julie cleared her throat. "Well, I'm sorry to say your facts are incorrect."

Everyone on the other side of the table—except for her superior, who grinned—raised their eyebrows. She knew she would shock them with her disagreement rather than her plea for forgiveness, attributing it to burnout, too many patients, insufficient time, or any excuse. But they hadn't anticipated her to fight back.

How can she word it to express doubt without placing blame on Carlos?

Just as she was about to continue, a commotion erupted as the door burst open.

"I apologize, Mr. Baker," the assistant pleaded.

He raised his hand and said, "It's okay, Mira. You may go now."

In disbelief, Julie stared at Rodney, who had interrupted her meeting. Did he not understand how important this was? He couldn't involve himself in this to protect her.

"I'm sorry, Mr. Baker," she began, but he shook his head and gestured for her to remain seated.

"Ah, Mr. White. I have given your team ample leeway in my hospital to protect Dr. Banks, but this is unacceptable. She is not in danger from anyone on this board or in this room."

Rodney glared at Mr. Baker until the man turned pale. "I'll decide that, but that's not why I'm here."

"Oh?" Mr. Baker tilted his head slightly. "Please share so we can keep running the hospital."

"You've got this all wrong," Rodney said, stepping beside her. "Dr. Banks didn't do anything wrong."

Julie felt like groaning. This wouldn't help her case.

"And how do you know this?"

Rodney put a hand on the back of her chair. "I was with Dr. Banks when she entered that order, and I know for a fact that she double-checked it."

"Did you see her input the medication into the tablet?"

He hadn't, and Julie knew it, so she questioned whether he would lie to protect her.

"No," he sighed. "But one of the students who followed her did see her enter the medication."

"Where is this student?"

"One moment." Rodney stepped away from her and opened the door.

What was he up to? She was curious about who would come to her aid, as she hadn't noticed if any students had seen her enter the information.

Marla walked into the room with her head down.

Julie narrowed her eyes. If Marla thought that lying would convince Julie to give her a passing grade, she was sadly mistaken.

"Tell them," Rodney urged.

Marla looked at Rodney with pleading eyes.

He nodded. "Go ahead and tell them."

"Look, Mr. White," Mr. Baker said, "we don't force students to express anything that might not be true, especially about their instructor."

Rodney faced the group of administrators. "Oh, you're going to love what she says." He turned back to Marla. "Go ahead and speak."

Marla's shoulders drooped. "I saw Dr. Banks enter the information correctly. She asked us to double-check if anyone was allergic to a medication we considered prescribing."

"Thank you—?" Mr. Baker paused. "What's your name?"

"Marla Rollins."

"Thank you, Ms. Rollins. You're excused."

Rodney rested his hand on Marla's shoulder. "She's not done yet."

"Do I really have to?" she begged Rodney.

He nodded. "Oh, yes, you definitely do."

"Okay." She sighed. "I watched Dr. Banks input the information, including her password. Later, I changed the order."

The board gasped in unison.

"Why would you do that if it might harm a patient?" Mr. Baker asked.

"Because," Marla glared at Julie, fury flashing in her eyes. "She was about to fail me."

Chapter Nineteen

DOC NOTICED JULIE was caught between gratitude and anger over his intervention. However, if he hadn't stepped in, she might have lost her job—a job that she cherished.

He also suspected it was linked to his not returning the previous evening. After returning home late, he hadn't wanted to wake her, knowing she needed to be refreshed for her hearing. He had tried to discuss Marla all morning, but she wouldn't engage. So, he had to surprise her, which he knew wouldn't be well received.

That was fine. He had plans for their evening that involved a lot of groveling. He knew that throughout their lives, there would be many times he'd upset her and would need to make amends, so he might as well practice now.

Julie turned to him as they stepped out of the SUV in front of his house. "Thank you." Then, she turned and walked into the building, not waiting for his reply. When he went inside, she was already climbing the stairs.

"What are you going to do?" Pup asked as he pulled out lunch meat and condiments from the refrigerator. The agent took bread from the shelf and opened a bag of chips. They didn't know how long the meeting would last, so they planned for a cold lunch, which none of the men objected to. Doc hoped Julie would feel the same way.

Doc wasn't sure what he would do that afternoon, but he figured he'd come up with something. "What do you mean?"

Casper snorted. "Yeah, as if you don't already know."

He couldn't be coy with his teammates, but who cared what they thought? Doc shrugged. "I'll come up with something."

"It's too bad you can't enjoy a picnic in the park," Grits said before taking a bite of his sandwich.

That sparked his idea. He remembered getting a collapsible picnic basket once, but he never used it. Now, where could he have hidden it?

Doc left the men behind and searched the top of the pantry, where he spotted the blue basket. Now, he needed a blanket, and they'd be all set.

He returned to the men. "Get out."

They paused with food in hand. "Out of the kitchen or out of the house?"

"The house."

Grits shook his head. "One of us needs to stay inside, Doc. You know that."

He did. "Okay, one stays inside." That scrapped the plans for the picnic in the living room. He would have to improvise. Both bedrooms had floor space, but which one should he choose?

The men shrugged, and Casper smiled. "Let us help you pack this up. I thought I saw some fruit in the refrigerator. Women like to take that on a picnic."

The men went to town, filled the basket for him, and surprised Doc with their generosity. He knew they cared for Julie, but this was beyond what he expected.

Other than Pup and Casey, the men headed out to patrol while Doc climbed the stairs carrying a basket of goodies.

He hoped this would regain her favor.

Choosing his room for the impromptu picnic, Doc spread a blanket on the floor and tossed down some pillows. He positioned the basket in the center, deciding not to open it yet. He would save that for Julie.

Once ready, he walked down the hall to Julie's door and knocked. "Julie?"

She opened the door slightly. "Yes?"

Doc let out a sigh. He had a lot of groveling to do. "It's lunchtime."

"I'm not hungry," she said, trying to shut the door, but he blocked it just in time.

"Let me take another shot at that. I've prepared lunch for us."

She looked down at his hands. "Where?"

He pointed to his bedroom. "In there."

Her eyes widened as if remembering last night when he had promised to return but left without a word, too eager to pursue the Marla lead that would clear her name.

"It's fine. I'll keep my hands to myself. It's just a picnic." He wouldn't say, "I promise," because he couldn't assure that he wouldn't touch her. But that would only happen if she wanted him to.

She nodded and opened the door wide enough to slip through. With his bedroom door left open, she followed him into the room.

"Oh, Rodney, this looks like fun."

He didn't think sitting on the hard floor would be enjoyable, but he'd make the best of it since she was with him. "I must admit," he said sheepishly, "the guys packed the basket. I'm not even sure what exactly is in it."

They both sat on the cushions.

Julie laughed, and his heart soared at the sound. "I hope they aren't trying to play matchmaker."

That hurt, but he wouldn't let it stop him. "I really believe they are."

When she started to speak, he raised his hand. "None of that. This is just lunch between friends. I owe you an apology, and I wanted to enjoy lunch while I groveled."

She opened the picnic basket and looked inside. "Grovel, huh?"

"Over sandwiches." He leaned back, watching her as she carefully selected items from the basket, arranging them just right. Her beauty captivated him, and he marveled at his good fortune. However, he also sensed the cloud of sadness that lingered over her.

Perhaps once he apologized, and they moved past his interruption during her meeting and his absence the night before, they could find their way back to being in each other's arms.

He knew she struggled with her attraction to him due to ethical concerns. Yet, he often reminded her that he had ended her role as his doctor long before they began—

what, dating? No, they hadn't dated unless you consider this a date. They had enjoyed moments of foreplay over the past few days and then fell into each other's arms, but they had skipped a lot. Maybe that's also what was holding her back.

"Sandwiches, chips, strawberries, grapes, and chocolate donuts."

Doc smiled. "The donuts were Pup's idea. He said that all women like chocolate, and that's all I had."

Julie chuckled. "There might be hope for that boy after all." She offered two sandwiches. "Ham or turkey?"

He knew she preferred turkey, so he chose ham.

As they unwrapped the sandwiches, he looked at her with intent. "So, have I been forgiven?"

She arched an eyebrow. "Is that what you call groveling? Choosing my least favorite sandwich?"

Doc shrugged, feeling small despite his size. "Well, yeah."

"Oh, Rodney," she said, then took a sip of water from a bottle. "You might want to look up 'groveling' online."

Well, hell. He'd actually have to apologize. After swallowing a bite of his sandwich, he said, "I'm sorry. Really sorry, Julie."

"For what, exactly?"

This was more difficult than he had anticipated. He disliked admitting his flaws, even to Julie. "I apologize for interrupting your meeting today, but I'm not sorry because you wouldn't allow me to share about Marla before we arrived."

"Wow. That's the saddest apology I've ever heard."

She popped a strawberry into her mouth, and he regretted not feeding it to her.

They had to get past this play on words to reach the makeup sex part. Or the "finally sex" part since they'd been interrupted the first time. Just thinking about it made his blood rush south, and his jeans tightened.

"All right, I'm sorry." He took a large bite of the sandwich to avoid arguing about why he shouldn't feel sorry and ruining the entire lunch.

"That's an improvement. So, what about the other one?"

He tilted his head, nearly forgetting that he still owed her another apology. "Julie, I'm sorry for not coming to your room when I got home. It was so late, and I didn't want to disturb you."

"You should have. You said you'd return to my bed but left me wanting."

Wanting, huh? That was a good sign. "If I could go back, I'd wake you up and ravage your body."

Julie laughed. "Now, that's an apology that's worth accepting."

"Does this mean I'm forgiven?"

She tapped her finger playfully on her chin. "I'm considering it." Then, she laughed and popped a grape into her mouth. Again, he wished he'd fed it to her. It was erotic watching her eat the fruit, even though he knew she wasn't trying to be sexy. She just…was.

Smiling, he beckoned with a crooked finger, inviting. "Come here."

"What about lunch? We haven't even gotten to the donuts yet," she teased.

"To hell with the donuts. Come here." He knew he could easily bridge the gap, but he wanted her to take the lead in completing what they had started the night before.

"Now that you put it that way, I'm coming." She pushed the food aside and slowly crawled toward him on her hands and knees, smiling the whole time.

What a seductive picture she created. He didn't conceal his gaze on her breasts as her shirt opened during the crawl. His mouth watered. He longed to taste her again.

"Before we start, you should know we won't be interrupted this time."

She halted a few feet away from him. "That's good to know."

His finger tenderly traced the line of her cheekbone and jaw. This woman held his heart, and he didn't know how to tell her without her thinking it was too soon. Did she believe in love at first sight? He hadn't until he met her. Even while injured and worried about his friend, he had fallen in love.

Thinking about Simon slightly shaded his meal, but he stayed resolute. This was about him and Julie.

His thumb grazed her lips, and she moaned. Oh yeah, he was taking her right now. He stood up suddenly. "Get up."

She jumped up with a questioning expression. "What? What happened?"

"Your room," he said, taking her hand and pulling her there.

"What about the food? Shouldn't we put it away?"

"We can get it later." Much later, if he had any say in

it.

She giggled and closed the door behind them as they stepped into her room. "So, big guy. What's this all about?"

"This." He pushed her against the door, pulling her arms above her head, and took her mouth hungrily. She didn't fight him. Instead, she rubbed herself against him, driving him mad with desire. Now that he had her, a nervous pulse skittered through him, making him wonder if she could feel his slight tremble.

Now, it's time for make-up sex.

Chapter Twenty

HE TOOK A deep breath, his tongue tracing the soft contours of her lips. They felt warm from his kiss. "I want you, Julie Banks." He lowered his lips and kissed the throbbing hollow at the base of her throat. "More than I've wanted any woman."

Her words nearly slipped past him with her head tilted to provide him access to her silky neck. "I feel the same."

He chuckled while kissing a trail back to her lips. "You want me more than any other woman?"

"Huh?" she asked breathlessly.

"Never mind." Reclaiming her lips, he let go of her arms and pulled her closer. His kiss was slow and gentle, and his tongue explored the depths of her mouth. He wanted to savor every inch of her.

"You're mine." He kissed her with a craving that masked his outward calm.

"I'm yours," she said after he pulled back from the kiss.

He lowered his hands and grabbed her waist, pulling her close against him. "I can't wait to taste every part of you."

She wrapped her arms around his neck, drawing him close as she pressed her lips to his. "What's holding you back?"

He growled, losing control.

Gently, he carried her to the bed, easing her down with his body following. His lips nibbled at her earlobe. As he traced a path down her neck, she moaned, making him wish he'd taken off his jeans before his dick went fully erect. As he ignited her passion, his own intensified.

"Clothes," he murmured, trailing his kisses over her sweater-clad breast.

He reached down, pulled her sweater over her head, and tossed it aside. Doc felt like he had won the lottery when she revealed her lace-covered bra with a front closure. He removed it from each arm and threw it away. Finally, he had those luscious breasts all to himself.

Doc caught her gaze, filled with desire. "You're beautiful."

With a coy smile, she reached for the hem of his shirt. "I believe you have too many clothes on."

After she pulled it over his head, she began exploring his chest. Each touch of her hands sent pleasure jolts through him. He captured her hands and pulled them above her head once more. He couldn't let her push him to the limit before she arrived.

His free hand softly traced a path across her abdomen and chest, pausing at her breast. His lips brushed against the rosy pink of her taut nipple.

She squirmed underneath him.

He knew she wanted to be free of his hold, but he needed to taste every inch of her without rushing or losing himself with an early orgasm. Slowly, his hand moved downward, skimming cither side of her body to her thighs. He'd have to let go of her arms if he wanted to move further. Besides, they needed to remove their jeans.

He climbed off her. "Shoes and pants."

She nodded and climbed out of bed.

They hastily took off their clothes, letting them fall to the floor without a second thought.

Afterward, she lay in the same spot where she had been initially.

Doc knelt on the bed, gazing at her body from head to toe, feeling a fire spreading from his groin to his heart. "I'm one lucky bastard," he murmured.

She smiled. "What did you say?"

He shook his head. "Nothing." Climbing onto her, he kissed the tip of her nose before pressing his mouth against hers in a soul-stirring kiss. Nothing prepared him for the fiery possession he felt for her. This woman would always be his.

He kissed her earlobe and whispered, "I'm going to love you like you've never experienced love before."

"Go ahead, then." She shifted beneath him.

He meant "love" as in "loving someone," but he thought she interpreted it as sex. Now wasn't the right time to clarify.

With deliberate intention, he kissed a trail down the center of her body, bypassing the curves he had already cherished. His resolve to explore every inch of her was unwavering, intoxicated by the alluring warmth of her silky skin.

He took a moment at her navel and glanced up at her. "Are you ready?"

With her hands in his hair, she smiled. "Yes." Her breathless response sent him into a frenzy of ecstasy.

He slid between her legs, his hands caressing the soft

insides of her thighs. A hot tide of passion raged as he gazed upon her. Leaning in, he licked her center, tasting her essence. Good God, she tasted amazing. No woman had ever tasted better.

As he licked her center, his thumb played with the taut nub waiting for him to suck. When she moaned, he felt the flames igniting within her.

"You taste better than I dreamed."

"I can't wait to taste you."

Yeah, that couldn't happen this time because he wouldn't be able to resist. "Next time."

She feigned a pout.

"Do you want me to spank your bottom?"

"Ooh, I've never done that. But not today."

He'd never spanked a woman during sex, either. He didn't see the point of adding pain to an act of raw passion.

He took her sensitive nub into his mouth, drawing a deep, shivering moan from her as her back arched off the bed. Her voice carried a new, urgent intensity, as if her body were on the brink of bursting.

With his fingers, he entered her and withdrew, imitating what he was about to do with her. And with his mouth, he worked her nub. In no time, she was begging him to stop.

"I want you inside me when I come."

He paused his ministrations. "Oh, you'll have that too."

"Promise?"

"Promise."

With that promise, she cried out, her body nearly lifting off the bed as he admired her radiant image of fire, passion, love, and pleasure.

"Rodney," she said as he climbed over her. "That was…."

He smiled as a surge of desire overtook him. He needed to have her right away.

As he grasped himself to enter her, he remembered. How could he forget? He'd never forgotten with a woman. "Condom," he growled. Why the hell hadn't he put any condoms in this room or kept one in his wallet? "Shit." His forehead touched hers.

Her legs brushed against his. "What's the matter?"

"I don't have one in here."

She let out a sigh. "I have one in my purse."

Later, he'd ask why she carried one, but now, he only cared when one was near. He jumped off the bed and riffled through her purse on the bedside table until he found it. He tore the package open and rolled the condom down his erect cock.

He climbed back onto the bed and covered her. "How are you?"

She played with his hair. "Utterly blissful."

"We're not finished."

"Good."

Reaching down, he positioned himself at her entrance and slowly surrendered to the passion and desire he felt for this woman as he entered her inch by inch, not wanting to hurt her by thrusting hard at first.

Once seated, he lowered his forehead to hers. "You know you're mine, right?"

"I will always be yours," she whispered.

Then he began to move, and together, they quickly found a rhythm that elevated his pleasure. Her eyes were closed, head thrown back, and her moans suggested she felt it just as deeply.

On each thrust, he neared the point of no return and hoped he'd given her enough pleasure to bring her to another orgasm. To help, he reached between them and toyed with her nub.

"Rodney," she whispered, "I'm going to come again."

As if he'd fight that. "Go. Fly."

During this rushing orgasm, she cried his name, and that brought him to the peak, and he came with an orgasm more potent than any he'd ever known.

Together, sweat shimmered on their bodies as they held each other for a moment before he lifted himself away. "Let me dispose of the condom. I'll be back shortly."

She moved seductively, her eyes closed. "Mmm."

Returning to bed, he lay beside her and propped himself on his elbow. "Rest, Julie. I'm here for you."

She rolled onto her side, and he pulled her back against him, wrapping his arm around her waist.

After noticing her change in breathing and being sure she was asleep, he allowed himself to do the same.

When Rodney woke, it was early evening. Wow, they had spent most of the day in bed. She must be hungry.

As he moved to leave and grab a snack, he accidentally woke her.

"Please don't go," she said, gazing into his eyes.

"I'll stay for as long as you want."

"I like that," she murmured, kissing him lightly. "I really like that."

"Then will you marry me?"

"Rodney, I haven't known you long enough to make such a leap into forever."

"Surely, our hearts have been dancing together since we met."

"I don't know you well enough to pledge my life to you."

"How many more excuses will you come up with when you know deep down that you truly want to be my wife?"

"Oh, so I do, huh?"

"Yes, Julie, you certainly do."

Her phone rang, interrupting their connection of love and attraction. She groaned. "I need to check it. It might be the hospital."

She rolled over and grabbed her phone from the nightstand. "Huh. It's Renee, Carlos's wife."

Doc stiffened, uncertain why since nothing they had uncovered suggested Renee as a suspect. Yet, he remained cautious. "Put it on speaker."

She raised an eyebrow at him but complied with his request. "Hi, Renee. Is everything all right?"

"No, it's not. You are deeply mistaken if you think you can ruin Carlos in court just to gain the practice. I won't allow that."

Chapter Twenty-One

JULIE'S EYES WIDENED in surprise at the threat from someone she had considered a friend—different from Laura and Stacy, but still a friend. Before Julie could respond, Renee abruptly ended the call.

Rodney jumped out of bed and quickly put on his jeans. "Get dressed. We're about to have company."

Feeling nervous and anxious, Julie followed the directions, putting on her jeans, sweater, and boots in case they decided to go out.

Rodney walked to the door and glanced back at her. "Ready?"

She nodded, and he opened it, shouting to Pup as he went, "Call in Grits and Casper, ASAP!"

By the time they reached the bottom of the stairs, the young agent was wrapping up a call. "What's up?"

Casey jumped up from her spot on the floor and ran over to Julie. She loved and petted the cute puppy, aware she was officially "at work" and should be overlooked.

"Hey, little one." She adored the pup and longed for one of her own. Yet, the demanding schedules of the hospital and clinic would mean leaving the dog mostly in someone else's care. She should probably get a cat or two. They didn't require her attention all the time. In fact, they didn't need her for most of the time. Julie chuckled.

Grits opened the front door, and he and Casper stepped inside. He glanced at Julie and nodded before turning back to Rodney. "What's up?"

Rodney grasped her hand and pulled her close. At first, she tried to pull away, but he held on tightly, and she realized he wanted them to see their connection.

"Julie just received a verbal threat from Garcia's wife. Have we investigated her?"

Grits nodded. "Devon has her on the list since she can access Garcia's account. It's possible she hired the hitman instead of Garcia."

The term "hitman" sent a chill down Julie's spine. Would Renee do something like that? It wasn't as if Carlos would go to jail if he lost the case. After all, this was a civil matter focused on money. They stood to lose a significant amount and possibly their share in the clinic if the settlement exceeded what they could afford.

"I want her re-evaluated," Rodney said. "That couple might be collaborating."

Casper stepped forward. "It doesn't make sense. It's just a civil case. It's about the money."

Julie's thoughts exactly. At least someone understood. "And the clinic," she added. "They're also suing the clinic, which means Carlos could lose his share."

Grits turned to her. "You know these people. Do you think that would be enough for them to try to kill you?"

Her instinct was to shake her head. "No." Then she

wondered if she really knew either of them well enough to understand the intricacies of their marriage and financial life.

"I don't think so, but I'm not sure." She frowned. "However, Ash is right."

The men gazed at Ash in disbelief, and he shrugged casually.

"This concerns money. Also, my testimony might not affect the case itself, so I don't believe they would try to harm me for that."

Rodney shook his head. "You'd be surprised at why people attempt to kill others. It can be for trivial reasons."

Julie had seen enough gunshot victims to agree with that. But still….

"We have a team assigned to Garcia."

Grits surprised Julie with that statement. She had no idea what they were doing other than protecting her, and maybe it was time to find out. "What else are you doing?"

"Let's sit down," Grits suggested.

The five of them sat while Casey relaxed at Julie's feet.

"Devon is searching for anomalies in the finances of everyone we've identified as potential suspects. Whoever it is, they aren't doing it themselves, so they must be paying someone and paying them quite a steep price."

That made sense to her, but she wondered how Devon managed to do this legally. Wasn't hacking a crime? She imagined he must have hacked because suspects wouldn't give investigators access to their financial records.

"And?" She wanted to know what they had found.

At this point, they should have uncovered something, especially if they were tailing Carlos.

"Jesse spoke with Dr. Garcia due to the large cash withdrawals but wouldn't clear him. We're monitoring him, nonetheless. Just in case."

"What about Renee? She might be withdrawing money and shopping or something." If the payments followed a pattern, then perhaps Renee was getting Botox. She was obsessed with the image she had to maintain as a successful surgeon's wife.

"We've considered her, but until now, there was no connection. This threat changes that. We need to show those withdrawals were made with the intent to harm you. But," he said, wincing, "the challenge is that cash transactions are hard to trace."

"So, what are you going to do?" This point frayed Julie's nerves. They were nowhere.

"We finally got a lead on the bomb signature from Chief Wise. We're sending a team over to the potential bomber's house now to beat the police. Chief gave us fifteen minutes to get the answers we need."

Julie couldn't believe how well the police had collaborated with this group. She hoped their efforts to seek answers wouldn't resort to violence.

"Who else have you been watching?"

Grits and Casper exchanged glances before looking back at her.

Grits sighed. "We're keeping an eye on your assistant and her brother."

Julie opened her mouth to speak, but Grits raised his hand, stopping her.

"We don't think either is involved. We believe that the damage to your office is unrelated to the bombing and shooting."

Julie sighed with relief. She dreaded the thought of Gary being so enraged that he would trash her office. He had deserved to be let go from the job. It had been difficult for Julie, but she had given him too many chances, and he disappointed her with everyone.

Julie's phone rang, and she glanced at the caller ID. It was Mary. She sent the call to voicemail. This was too important to ignore, and Mary had nothing urgent to say. She'd leave a message.

"Go on," Julie encouraged.

Grits nodded. "We talked to a few other surgeons on staff to see if anyone was jealous enough about your potential promotion to act on their anger. They all checked out."

Once more, Julie sighed in relief. She would hate to believe that the people who would soon be her staff would want to harm her.

"I hate to say this," Grits said, "but we're uncertain. That's why we want to keep the protection detail going until we sort this out for you."

But how long would that take? Would it require another attempt on her life to draw out the would-be killer? She mentally shook her head. She didn't want that to happen.

"Do you think the person who made the bomb will reveal who paid them?"

Casper shook his head. "I doubt it, but it's worth a shot."

Great. They were back to square one, and now only Carlos—and Renee—have potentially engaged killers for hire.

Julie racked her brain, figuring out who might hold a grudge against her. "Did you check anyone with a problem with my surgical skills?"

Grits nodded. "It was a pretty short list. You do an exceptional job, Doc. Even those who lost someone appreciate the efforts you made to save their loved ones."

Julie worked tirelessly and continuously read to stay updated on the latest surgical techniques to save as many lives as possible. She understood she couldn't save everyone, and it devastated her. However, some patients came to her too late, or their injuries were beyond repair.

"I suppose that's why they're looking to appoint you as chief of surgery at such a young age," Pup remarked.

It was amusing to hear Pup talk about being young. What was the kid's age? Twenty, perhaps? Maybe a bit older, but definitely under twenty-five.

"Thank you." Whenever she received a compliment about her position, she felt embarrassed, as if she shouldn't have it, despite knowing she possessed the surgical and leadership skills necessary to lead a successful team of surgeons.

Her phone rang again. It was Mary. She sent it to voicemail once more. Mary understood there were times Julie couldn't answer, like when she was with a patient or in surgery. Well, this situation was equally important.

Grits and Casper exchanged glances, and Casper nodded in response.

Grits turned to Julie. "So, we looked into Stacy and

Laura, too."

Julie jumped up. "Why are you looking at my friends? They have nothing to do with this!"

Rodney took her hand, gently guiding her back onto the sofa beside him. "Hey, just relax and listen to us."

Relax? Her pulse quickened at their audacity to check up on her friends.

Without missing a beat, Grits continued, "But we still haven't cleared either of them."

Julie frowned, knitting her brows into a deep V. "What do you mean by that?"

"Well, both of them tend to live beyond their means," Grits responded, "so they might be able to hire someone if needed."

"No! They wouldn't." Julie was furious now, and her anger was a force to be reckoned with regarding her friends.

"Julie," Doc said, rubbing her palm with his thumb. "Could you just listen for a moment?"

She let out an exasperated huff, looking as if she were a stubborn kid caught doing something wrong. Yanking her hand away from Rodney, she crossed her arms tightly over her chest.

"All right, go ahead," she said to Grits, motioning for him to continue.

Grits cleared his throat and said, "Well, the good news is we didn't find any withdrawals that match either of the incidents."

Incident? Someone had tried to kill her, and he was so relaxed about it.

"Of course not. They would never come after me,"

she snapped back.

"Sometimes, it's the people we least expect," Casper interjected.

"Who else are you investigating?" Julie asked, eager to redirect the focus. The thought of her friends being capable of such a terrible act made her feel nauseous.

"Your students." Grits shifted in his seat. "That's how we found out about Marla changing the order."

Thank goodness they found that out. The school expelled Marla, and Julie knew she was blaming her instead of taking responsibility for her actions. Could she have wanted to kill her? She didn't care if she killed an innocent man.

"Is it Marla?"

Grits shook his head. "No, but we'll monitor her for retaliation concerning expulsion. We can't trust her after she attempted to kill someone and tried to pin the blame on you."

Julie felt her heart warm at the thought that these men would keep her safe. She hadn't even hired them—though she would pay them—and they went above and beyond.

"Thank you," she said, glancing at Grits and then Casper. "Please give my thanks to the team."

The men smiled. "Doc," Casper said, "they'll be happy to hear that."

A thought struck Julie. "By the way—" She flushed with embarrassment but continued. "Thank you for packing the picnic lunch."

"Our pleasure," Grits said.

She turned to Pup. "Especially the chocolate." They

hadn't eaten any, but she wanted the kid to know she appreciated his effort, which was rewarded with a cute blush on the agent's face.

"So," she inquired, "where does that leave us?"

Grits sighed. "Not in a good place. But while Devon checks the records, we'll be your bodyguards."

"Court has been rescheduled for tomorrow." She gulped, her stomach knotting. "Do you think someone will try something before that?"

Rodney nodded. "If it's about the lawsuit, then yes."

She finally focused entirely on him. Julie loved this man, feeling it with all her heart and soul. She didn't want him to get hurt while trying to protect her, but what choice did she have? If she tried to go alone, she might die. At least these men had weapons to keep her safe.

Her phone rang again, and she couldn't believe it. Mary was calling once more. Why hadn't she just left a message like usual? But since it was the third time, it might be something Mary thought was important. Since they had ended the conversation, she said, "Excuse me."

Standing, she walked to the kitchen to answer the call. "Hello, Mary. Is everything okay?"

"Dr. Banks, you should come to the office. I discovered something important for you to see."

Chapter Twenty-Two

THE FOLLOWING DAY, anxiety infused Julie. First, she had to stop by the office to review Mary's evidence and head to the courthouse for the trial.

Rodney, who had spent most of the night with her, sat beside her in the SUV. He worried about Mary since she had been secretive about what she had found, but Julie trusted that Mary wouldn't hurt her. Even though Gary might have been upset about his termination, Mary didn't show any reaction. She had asked if she could work for Julie instead of Carlos. Still, Julie realized the importance of avoiding office politics in a small workplace, so they divided her responsibilities until Mary took over for Gary. That had been months ago.

As she fidgeted with her hands, Rodney gently clasped them in his own. "It's okay. I'll be there."

"What?" She shook her head. "Oh, no, it's not the office. It's the courthouse I'm most anxious about. All my problems may have revolved around it."

Rodney smiled. "I will be there too."

Grits turned from the front seat. "Dr. Garcia is also going to the office before court."

"Shit." Rodney clasped her hand tightly.

Julie sighed, concerned about this development. "Now is the perfect time to tell him about his wife. Maybe he doesn't realize that she might be behind it all."

"Julie, we still haven't cleared him," Rodney protested.

She waved her other hand dismissively. "I understand you're worried about Carlos, but now that I've considered it, I don't believe it's him. I think it's Renee. She has access to his money, so she could easily have done whatever she thought was necessary to protect her husband."

"They both have the motive and the means." Rodney lifted her hand to his mouth and kissed it. "Just don't be alone with him."

"I won't," she lied, fully aware that she planned to tell Carlos about Renee's call and potential involvement. Julie knew she would go to great lengths to protect Rodney, but she refused to cross the line into murder. In fact, she set boundaries on many things, but murder was one line she would never cross.

Rodney chuckled. "Somehow, I just don't believe you. Never close the door behind you when you're with him. I want to always keep eyes and ears on you."

She could do that. She nodded. "Okay." Then, she leaned over and rested her head on his shoulder. Closing her eyes, she breathed in his fresh cologne and relaxed. All would be fine now that Rodney was beside her.

Last night, he didn't mention the marriage question again, leaving her unsure if he was joking about it like before or being serious this time. Everything felt so sudden, yet it didn't. Things had never felt so right with someone. Her heart belonged to him. She was in love with him.

Although there was no urgent reason to rush into marriage, she felt at ease with the idea, provided she had a few months to carefully plan specific details, such as the design of her dream dress. She didn't envision a lavish wedding. Her closest friends were Stacy and Laura, so she planned to have just two bridesmaids. Naturally, Stacy would take on the role of maid of honor. She recognized that this decision might be difficult for Laura. Still, deep down, she trusted her friend would eventually come to understand, especially when presented with the charming men Rodney would bring to the wedding reception.

She had genuinely expected her life to follow the typical pattern of surgeons marrying fellow surgeons or a trophy husband, only to end in divorce a few years later. This was partly why she had never taken anyone seriously. That wasn't the life she wanted. She wished for the love she felt for Rodney to infuse her entire life.

"What made you smile?" he whispered.

She raised her head and looked into his eyes. "You."

"Great! So, when are we going to set the date?"

A laugh bubbled up from deep within, sending all her nerves out the window. "You never give up, do you?"

"Not with you," he said, kissing her forehead. "Never with you."

She welcomed his comfort and the words that made her heart race.

He leaned into the curve of her neck and whispered,

"I love you, Julie Banks."

Her heart soared to new heights. She believed he might, given that he'd asked for marriage, but he hadn't said those words before. It was a strange time to process his love, but she thought any time would do.

"Do you love me?" he softly asked in her ear.

She nodded. "Yes," she replied, breathless.

"So, are you going to say yes to my proposal?"

Rodney definitely wasn't the kind of guy to propose on one knee. He'd ask while injured, while in a hospital bed, and, well, she'd lost count of how many times he'd asked.

"I'll think about it." Her heart swelled with the promise of a commitment—one she knew would endure a lifetime. They shared something that most couples lacked—true love.

He kissed the hollow of her throat and squeezed her hand. "That's all I ask."

Cowboy drawled, "Sorry to interrupt the festivities, but we're here. The other team has arrived, which means Dr. Garcia is here too."

Reality loomed over her happiness, yet she refused to let it be taken away. She was resolute in her desire to become Rodney's wife very soon.

Julie waited as they cleared the clinic. "Everything has been checked except for Dr. Garcia's office. The door is closed, and the team mentioned he just arrived."

"Julie," Rodney said before letting her out of the SUV, "you are not to go near that office without me."

She nodded. "Okay." However, she didn't care whether Rodney was present or not. He could watch her entire conversation with Carlos for all she cared. She just needed to have it.

As Julie walked into the office, Mary seemed nervous, which made her worry. What was going on? Rodney must have noticed, too, because he moved closer to her side.

After ensuring that Carlos's door was closed, Julie greeted the assistant. "Good morning, Mary. I'm sorry for not having much time, but I'm curious about what was so important."

Mary glanced at Carlos's door and swallowed. "It's just—" She paused, looking at Rodney. Then she gulped. "I'm sorry. HIPAA."

Julie understood that it involved patient information. She turned to Rodney. "Julie and I are going to my office." Without waiting for his approval, she led the assistant to her office and closed the door. Anticipating Rodney's worry, she opened the blinds on the small window to the outer office so he could see inside.

She approached her chair and invited Mary to sit. "All right, Mary, what's on your mind?"

Mary fidgeted. "I was clearing out the patient billing files and saw that some of Dr. Garcia's files were mixed in with yours, so I began to organize them. That was when I noticed this." She handed Julie a set of paperwork.

She anticipated more elaboration. However, Mary fell silent, her hands clasped in her lap and her head bowed.

"I should have noticed it earlier but never checked the old bills after Gary left."

Julie felt overwhelmed as she looked down at the

stack of patient bills. She didn't have time to comprehend what Mary was trying to show her. Since she didn't manage the billing, she had expected the assistants to perform their duties correctly. Mary and Gary were trained in medical billing and coding.

"What am I looking at?"

Mary stood and approached the side of the desk, surprising Julie. She restrained herself from being overly skittish. There was nothing to fear from Mary, especially since Rodney was outside the door.

The assistant indicated a location on the first patient's bill. "Here," she said, then directed to another location, adding, "and here."

Julie noticed it right away, and anger surged through her veins. "Are they all the same?"

Mary stepped back and returned to her seat. "I'm afraid they are." She looked pleadingly at Julie. "I swear I had nothing to do with this. It was when Gary oversaw billing."

Needing a moment alone, she dismissed Mary. "Thank you. I'll handle it from here."

Mary stood up. "I'm sorry."

Julie nodded, recognizing that the girl was seeking her forgiveness. "I understand, Mary. I also know you wouldn't do something like this."

As Mary left, Rodney walked in. "Is everything okay?"

"No." She put the bills in a folder to deal with later, but her temper was on the verge of getting the best of her.

"Anything you can discuss?"

Julie glanced up and squinted. "The jerk is involved in Medicare fraud. He's jeopardized our clinic one time too many."

Rodney whistled and sank into the chair opposite her desk. "What are you going to do?"

Rolling her shoulders to ease the tension, she sighed deeply. "Whatever it takes to protect the clinic." She wouldn't lie under oath or break the law, but she would discover a way to separate Carlos from the clinic.

She needed to find a way to buy him out. Perhaps she could sell her house and buy something more affordable. Even better, they could stay at Rodney's place. She loved it there.

She tapped her finger on the top of the file, her mind swirling with possibilities to save the clinic and considering how it could end because of Carlos. Her anger reached new heights.

The vibration of a phone caught her attention.

Rodney smiled. "It's mine. Let me step out and take this." He went into the outer office, down the hall, and answered the call. Julie knew he could still see her office from where he stood, which made her feel safe.

But she didn't feel secure or at ease in her job. She had reached her limit.

Grasping the folder, she stood up and took determined steps toward Carlos's closed door. She knew Rodney could see her, so she didn't worry about being in danger. Besides, she would leave the door open as he'd asked.

Mary jumped up. "There's something else you need to know," she said anxiously. "His latest mistress is with him."

Chapter Twenty-Three

FUMING AND INDIFFERENT to whether he was with the Queen of England, Julie stormed up to Carlos's door and flung it open without knocking. "Carlos—"

She couldn't take in anything more. The sight before her stole the breath from her lungs. She quickly shut the door to keep anyone from seeing Laura in her partner's married arms.

"Laura?" She couldn't fully comprehend what she was witnessing. She knew Carlos had been unfaithful to Renee, which made her feel nauseous, but she never expected Laura to become involved with a married man. And Carlos, of all people.

"Julie," Carlos said as he moved closer to her.

"Stop right there," she said, doubting her decision to close the door.

Just as she was about to reach back and open it, Laura breezed by and locked it with a quick click. "No, we don't need your guard dog to settle this."

"Settle what? If you two want to fool around, that's fine with me. I'd rather not have known, though." The words hung in the air, heavy with unspoken tension. As she turned to leave, she felt a sharp tug—Laura had caught her arm in a fierce grip.

"Not until we have a little chat."

Julie's heart raced as she yanked her arm free and narrowed her eyes. The room was filled with a pulsing silence. "Yes, I need to talk to Carlos—not you." The finality in her voice hung in the air, thick with the promise of confrontation.

Laura walked back to Carlos and took his hand. "You can say whatever you want in front of me. Isn't that right, darling?"

Julie's stomach twisted in knots at the endearment, her unease growing with Laura's unsettling demeanor. Something felt off, urging her to leave. "It involves HIPAA, so no, I can't talk in front of you," she said, her voice barely a whisper as she turned toward the door.

"Do you mean that little billing issue?" Laura's voice dripped with venom. "I should've seen that brat outside would dig it up. She's getting too nosy for her own good."

Julie felt her heart drop, disbelief washing over her. Was Laura really confessing to her role in Carlos's Medicare fraud?

With a heavy sense of dread, she slowly turned to face them again. "What did you say?"

Carlos cleared his throat nervously. "Now, Laura—"

But Laura interrupted him with a sharp laugh, giving Julie goosebumps. "No, we knew she'd discover it, eventually. We prepared for this. We talked about what needed to be done."

What needed to be done? The implications hung in the air, dark and foreboding, as a cold shiver ran down

Julie's spine. As in…..

"Were—" Julie cleared her throat, the words nearly choking her. "Were you two responsible for trying to kill me?" Panic surged through her veins as she remembered Rodney's warnings about Carlos. Where was he? Moments stretched like an eternity as she waited for him to burst in and rescue her. Surely, he must have noticed her absence. Mary would have told him where she was. Right?

Laura pulled her hand away from Carlos's, her expression changing ominously. She walked over to her purse, and in an instant, she pulled out a gun.

Julie's heart raced, the pulse echoing in her ears. She had never seen this ruthless side of Laura, and it chilled her to the core. How had she been so blind? Would her friend actually pull the trigger?

A chilling reality enveloped her—Laura had already demonstrated her readiness to inflict pain. Why wouldn't she take it further now?

With trembling hands, Julie slowly raised them, patient records spilling to the floor like the remnants of her shattered trust. "Laura—"

"I don't really want to harm you, but I will if I must. Scream, and I shoot you. Attempt to leave before we've settled this, and I'll shoot you."

"Laura, sweetheart," Carlos urged. "Honestly, there has to be another way."

"No!" Laura snapped. "There isn't any."

"But the men are outside. They'll hear us and come in here," Carlos whispered urgently, the tension in the air palpable. "You'll never get away with this."

"We will," Laura asserted, her voice oozing with confidence. "Because Julie knows how to survive. She's smart enough to stay silent in court today and ignore the billings."

"Why?" Julie's voice trembled, filled with fear. "Why go through all this?" Her heart raced as she contemplated the drastic measures she might take to buy herself a little more time for Rodney to realize she was missing.

Laura glided back to Carlos, an unsettling smirk tugging at her lips. "Carlos is abandoning his wife, and we're running away to Bora Bora."

Suddenly, Julie noticed Carlos's shoulders tense. The flicker of panic in his eyes revealed more than he intended. A bubble of laughter escaped her, trapped in the moment's absurdity. How could it be so darkly humorous?

Laura's gaze sharpened, cutting through the silence. "What's so damn funny?"

Julie lowered her arms, her laughter fading but a sly smile remaining. "Is he now?" She turned toward Carlos, her voice a whisper yet filled with intent. "I suppose she's the reason for those large cash withdrawals from your account so Renee wouldn't catch on."

Carlos nodded grimly, his eyes narrowing as tension lingered in the air.

"And," Julie said, her voice steady yet tinged with anticipation, "let me guess. The Medicare fraud was Laura's idea." This notion had a twisted sort of logic. Laura's position in medical billing provided her with the ideal inside track for such deception.

"Honestly?" Julie continued, her expression steely. "I don't care what shady schemes you two come up with. My focus is solely on saving this clinic."

"Right," Laura spat, venom lacing her words. "Miss Goody Two-Shoes."

Julie chuckled darkly. "If you were truly going to shoot me, you would have done it by now. But here we are, and as I see it, you don't have an escape plan." She could sense the gravity of the moment shift, aware that Rodney was lurking outside with more men at both the front and rear entrances.

Laura's expression contorted into a grimace. "I told you she was smart, darling," she said, her voice tinged with unease.

Carlos fixed his gaze on Laura, an unspoken decision hanging in the balance. "Let's just let her go. We have more than enough money. We could skip the court appearance and vanish on a private jet." A crackling silence enveloped them.

Julie tilted her head to the side. "Why are you lying to her, Carlos? You've told every woman you cheated on Renee with that you'd leave her and go to Bora Bora?"

Laura's bravado wavered. "It's different for me. He truly means it. Don't you, darling?"

Carlos nodded. "Of course. Definitely."

As Laura shifted her focus to Carlos, Julie dashed for the door. It swung open just before she could unlock it, almost hitting her in the face. She stepped back as an enraged Rodney stormed in, weapon drawn.

****

"Put it down, Laura." Doc's commanding voice

sliced through the tense atmosphere, freezing everyone in their tracks. Every muscle in his body was tensed, anticipating the next move.

Laura quickly pivoted, aiming the gun back at Julie, then dashed behind Carlos, using his sturdy frame as a shield. "I promise I won't hurt your precious Julie if you let us walk away unharmed." Her voice dripped with menace.

Doc's expression grew serious. "Julie, stand behind me."

Incredibly, she obeyed, and he felt her grip the back of his shirt. Then, he sensed her peering over his shoulder. He wanted to shake either his head or hers.

Laura tightened her finger on the trigger, shifting her focus to him. The gravity of the situation clawed at his insides—one wrong move and someone could get hurt. Desperation surged as Doc confronted a cornered animal, with fear slipping away and being primed for violence.

"Julie," Laura hissed, her eyes narrowing with a menacing glint, "come here, or your lover pays the price."

The word "lover" pierced the atmosphere like a match struck in darkness, igniting a flame of dread deep within his chest. Had she revealed their secret that quickly? He didn't care who uncovered the truth, but the mere thought of this woman knowing sent a shiver down his spine, leaving him feeling exposed and almost filthy.

"No, Julie," Doc warned, narrowing his eyes as he instinctively pulled Julie closer. He then shot a wary glance at Laura, whose presence felt like a brewing storm.

"Don't underestimate me. I mean every word," Laura declared, her tone infused with a chilling certainty.

Tension crackled in the air, thick and suffocating, as he sensed Julie's body shift, a sign of the storm brewing between them.

"I'm sorry," she whispered, her voice trembling, a fragile thread of fear as she slipped from his protective embrace. "She won't hurt me. But you...I fear for you."

"Julie, no! Have you forgotten what she's done? This isn't a game. She didn't just threaten you—she plotted your death!" His voice broke with urgency, the weight of impending doom looming over them both.

"Now," Laura hissed, her voice low and filled with chilling menace as Julie approached, "you'll let us leave with her. I'll release Julie once we're at the airport, free and clear."

Doc's heart pounded. Every instinct screamed at him not to trust Laura and Carlos, especially with Laura wielding that gun like a deadly extension of her will. He had drilled into Julie the importance of staying out of a kidnapper's car—he could only hope she remembered that lesson now.

"I'll go with you," Julie stated firmly.

The confidence in her voice twisted like a dagger in his gut. Every nerve in his body screamed for action as Doc felt the weight of the moment—his gun arm dropped helplessly when Julie stepped in front, blocking his shot at Laura.

"I'll be fine," she insisted, but the clarity of her words felt fragile, resonating with uncertainty in the dense air.

"Julie, no," his voice pierced through the urgent tension laced with rising panic.

"Julie, yes," Laura retorted, her tone cold and conclusive, allowing no room for defiance. "Now, step aside and let us through."

Every second felt stretched, and all Doc could think was that rescue would come swiftly if Laura's finger didn't slip on the trigger. When he finished his call with Devon—where he'd identified Laura as Carlos's lover and the recipient of the cash withdrawals—and confirmed that Laura was in the office—he set the men in motion and sent Nemo to the rooftop across the street.

After what seemed like an eternity, his fingers hesitantly loosened their grip on the gun as he holstered it with quiet determination. He needed to allow the men time to get into position.

"Carlos," Laura said, her voice low and sharp like a knife. "You take the back."

As they passed him, Julie forced a smile and a nod. She was trying to convey that she trusted him and the team. He hoped her delaying—if that were indeed her intention—wouldn't lead to harm before they could rescue her from this nightmare.

He shifted, his brow furrowed, as he subtly moved toward them, uncertainty flickering in Julie's eyes.

Laura swiftly yanked the gun from Julie's back, the cold barrel now pressing against her temple. "Stop! I mean it. I won't hesitate to pull the trigger."

Doc raised his hands in a gesture of surrender. "Let me go first. I'll clear the way of the men."

Laura nodded. "Go on. Just remember, I'm keeping an eye on you. No funny business."

Doc moved in front of Julie, hovering just out of her

reach.

As they passed through the looming shadows of the open door, darkness enveloped them as they turned right toward the entrance. His voice projected, cutting through the tension. "Stand down!" he commanded to the men they met.

Every man froze, hands poised over their weapons, eyes fixed on Laura. The threat was palpable in the air. Each second felt like an eternity, and every breath was heavy with uncertainty. The air crackled with tension, and every heartbeat was a countdown.

As they inched closer to Carlos's vehicle, a chilling wave of doubt washed over Doc. Where was Nemo? No one spoke over the communication system. He needed to hear that Nemo was in position.

"Stop," Laura commanded, her voice cutting through the tension like a knife. "You can join your men."

Doc hesitated, nodded slowly, and stepped aside, his heart continuing to hammer in his chest.

The parked vehicle filled him with dread. How could Julie possibly avoid getting into it?

Regardless of the situation, he couldn't trust that they would leave Julie alone. The stakes were too high—her very freedom was at risk.

With Julie standing firm in front and Carlos looming ominously behind, Laura radiated an aura of invincibility.

"Don't do it, Julie. Don't get in the car," Doc pleaded, hoping she was stalling and not utterly terrified.

To his delight, she remained frozen.

"Get in," Laura commanded, her low, menacing voice echoing ominously and sending shivers down his spine.

"No."

Laura pressed the gun against Julie's temple. "I said, get in."

Doc tensed, eager to jump into the fray but aware it could get Julie killed. Where the hell was Nemo?

"And I said no." She remained defiant.

"This isn't just a game, Julie," Laura said, her voice low and menacing. "I will kill you—and your lover."

Something had happened to Nemo. Had he run into an issue bringing a sniper rifle into the building? They'd checked this possibility with the owners, but had an employee panicked?

Doc needed to act. He couldn't let Julie get into that vehicle.

Then, he heard the blessed shot a moment after blood spattered on the vehicle, Julie and Carlos. Laura crumpled forward onto Julie's body, causing her to fall to the ground.

"Julie!" he shouted. Instantly, he was at her side, kneeling and assisting her from under Laura's body. He heard a flurry of footsteps and realized Carlos was being restrained. Julie was safe.

"Nemo?" she inquired.

Doc nodded. "Yes, sweetheart." He pulled her into his arms, tighter than ever, and never let her go. "Don't ever do that again. You took nine lives off me."

As she embraced him, his fear dissolved. This woman meant the world to him.

She glanced at him and softly said, "Aren't you going to ask?"

With a trembling hand, he wiped her cheek, a splash of blood on his palm, then chuckled. "Of course I am. I was going to wait, but Julie Banks, will you marry me?"

"Yes!" She kissed him with an intensity she had never shown before.

At last, she was his.

Epilogue

DOC STOOD AT the altar with Grits, marking six months of anticipation and longing. Today was not merely a celebration of love—it represented hope, resilience, and the promise of a future with Julie, who had emerged from the shadows of past turmoil. Her career had withstood challenges, including the fallout from a previous partnership that forced her to rebuild her professional life, leading to her promotion to chief of surgery.

During the agonizing wait between ops, Doc gathered the courage to visit Simon's family. His heart ached as he offered his deepest apologies for not being able to keep Simon safe. The family, weary from grief yet full of understanding, gently reassured him that they didn't hold him responsible. They recognized the harsh realities of life in a dangerous city like Baltimore, yet Simon's unwavering spirit had led him to request this visit. He wanted to share his final moments with those he loved before he succumbed to the unforgiving grip of cancer—a devastating truth he hadn't dared to reveal to them until now.

With her unwavering support, Julie became his beacon of hope, guiding him through the shadows of his past and helping him to heal his wounds. She nurtured his spirit and taught him the power of forgiveness, allowing him to finally embrace the light and move forward in life with a heart full of compassion for himself.

But today, as he looked at his gathered friends and family—Casper and Nettie, Romeo and Daisy Mae, Boss and Sugar, Ballpark and Moira, Cowboy and LizzyBeth, Pup with Casey at his feet, Speedy, Nemo, Stone, and the Hamilton family with their lively children—Doc felt the weight of their support and Simon's spirit. Each face symbolized their challenges and the bonds they had created through shared experiences in the field, where camaraderie was crucial.

But amid the joy, an unsettling presence lingered. Pup gazed warily at the new female handler on the Alpha team who joined the ranks. Although she had once excelled as a top SWAT dog handler, her arrival sparked unease among the team. In a world where trust was crucial, any newcomer deserved scrutiny.

The Russian twins loomed over the occasion like a cloud, reminding them of the dangers surrounding them. Their appearance signaled that deep-cover operations might follow—an unavoidable reminder that their precarious reality could overshadow every celebration in their lives.

Doc's commitment to Julie grew increasingly clear in this moment of joy, intertwined with uncertainty. Their love story transcended the ordinary. It was a tapestry woven with threads of sacrifice, loyalty, and shared hope in adversity.

After all the insights, he cleared his throat and looked at Grits, one of the few single agents. "So, who do you think will be next?"

Grits laughed and said, "Definitely not me!"

Doc raised an eyebrow. "Oh, come on. It could be you."

Grits waved his hand dismissively. "No way. I tried the whole love thing once, and it was a disaster. It's just not my scene."

"That doesn't mean there isn't someone out there for you," Doc countered.

Grits shook his head. "You know what? I'm betting on Pup. I feel this new handler will give him tough competition."

Doc shifted his gaze to the crowd and, sure enough, spotted Pup giving the new handler a fierce glare while the handler shot back the same vibe. "Wow, that's going to be chaos."

Grits laughed once more. "Do you think it will be hell for them or us?"

Doc replied with a smile, "Probably both."

As music filled the air, Doc's heart soared with anticipation. At long last, the moment he had been waiting for finally arrived.

Gracefully dressed in a lavender gown, Stacy glided down the aisle, her radiant smile contagious. With every step, her gaze appeared to seek Grits, as if she were sharing a secret joy meant solely for him.

The melody shifted when Stacy took her place, stirring a whirlwind of emotions in Doc. Yet, as he glimpsed Julie, calmness washed over him like a soothing balm.

Julie glided up the aisle, her broad smile lighting up the room. She wore the exquisite white lace gown she had designed, which seemed to encapsulate the light and essence of their love.

She promised him that she had shopped at Madison and Rylee's lingerie store for their wedding night. The phrase "wedding night" filled him with longing and desire for the woman he loved. She would be his equal, by his side, for a lifetime.

The clergy cleared his throat. "Are we all set?"

He and Julie nodded. "Yes," they replied together.

From the tender words of "Dearly Beloved" to the heartfelt declaration, "I now pronounce you husband and wife," Doc found himself lost in daydreams of a beautiful future with Julie. He envisioned the laughter of their children filling their home and imagined a life overflowing with love, joy, and endless possibilities that awaited them together.

In the reception line, Doc greeted everyone while listening to his teammates' playful banter and their wives' warm wishes. It seemed they had all made wise choices in life and love.

He wished the same for his teammates, including the new Charlie team he had barely met before they were deployed overseas. After their return, there would be ample time to get to know them.

Cowboy shook his hand and turned to Julie. "So, what do we call you two? Doc and Doc could get confusing."

Julie smiled a smile that lit up his insides. "You may call me Julie. As for him," she gestured to her new husband, "you can call him Doc."

"Deal." He turned to his wife. "This is LizzyBeth, and this little tyke is Ethan." He rested his hand on the head of a boy LizzyBeth brought into their marriage. Cowboy treated the child as his own. "And," he turned to his wife, who nodded, "we have one on the way."

"Congrats, man," Doc said as Julie hugged LizzyBeth and congratulated her.

"Are you sure you're prepared for diaper changes and feedings at two in the morning?" Doc asked.

The agent tilted his cowboy hat back on his head. "I suppose I'll have to be."

Doc chuckled at the idea of Cowboy changing diapers. From what he knew, no parent was ever truly ready for that. They learned as they went along.

The groups moved forward, and finally, they were ready to cut the cake, dance, and enjoy whatever else was planned for this gathering. Doc just tagged along, hoping they could slip away unnoticed.

Both families from Kissimmee, Florida, attended and quickly formed a friendship. One of Julie's military brothers couldn't get leave, but they planned to send him a video of the wedding and reception.

When it was time for the toast, Doc was pleased to learn that Matt would be making the toast.

"To Doc and Julie," Matt said, holding a glass of champagne. "Get comfortable being uncomfortable—"

Doc nearly burst into laughter when he heard Matt use a Navy SEAL saying in his toast. Next, he expected

Matt to say, "Enjoy the suck" or "The only easy day was yesterday." But Matt surprised him.

"Ladies and gentlemen, if you would raise your glasses—tonight, we celebrate a warrior, a brother, and now, a husband. I've had the honor of standing beside this man through some of life's most challenging moments. I've witnessed his strength, loyalty, and ability to adapt and overcome—qualities that make him an outstanding SEAL and HIS agent and the kind of man who would move mountains for the woman he loves.

"To Julie—congratulations. You've tamed a warrior. If anyone can keep him in check, it's you. He may have been trained for combat, but we all know he's now answering to a higher command in this partnership.

"Like the Teams, marriage is about trust, loyalty, and always having each other's backs. Knowing this man, I have no doubt he'll be the kind of husband who stands firm in the fight, never gives up, and always finds his way back home—to you.

"Here's to a lifetime filled with love, laughter, and success on our missions. *Hooyah!*"

Doc raised his glass. "Hooyah!" was echoed by all the former naval agents on the teams.

Julie lifted her glass to him and smiled. "I love you."

He leaned in and kissed her gently on the lips. "And I love you."

They linked arms and sipped champagne while the photographer took pictures.

Doc wondered how long he would endure this dog-and-pony show. He had always believed that the wedding was for the bride and groom, while the reception was for the guests.

When Doc saw the new FBI Director, Steven Hicks, with the Russians behind him, speaking with Jesse and Devon, he realized their fun would be short-lived. At least he'd be in Bora Bora with his new wife when whatever was about to happen with the Russians unfolded.

Unfortunately, this meant he would miss the interaction between Pup and the new handler, which he hated. However, he thought their tense relationship would still be active when he returned.

"Now, wife," he said tenderly, a warm smile lighting up his face as he gazed at Julie.

"Yes, my husband?" she whispered.

"Are we ready to depart?"

"We still have a few photographs to take."

He drew her closer, feeling their warmth envelop each other, igniting an electric connection. "Are we ready to embark on this journey?"

She leaned into him, their chemistry intensifying, causing him to clench his jaw against the wave of desire. The thought of being caught off-guard by the other agents was enough to make him blush.

"Yes, I believe we are."

"Then, let's go."

ABOUT THE AUTHOR

SHEILA KELL writes about romantic men who leave women's hearts pounding with a happily ever after built on memorable, adrenaline-pumping stories. She is a four-time winner of the Readers' Favorite Book Award for romantic and contemporary suspense.

As a Southern girl who has left behind her days with the United States Air Force and as a University Vice President, she can usually be found on the Florida coast with her family and cats. When she isn't writing, you can find Sheila with her nose in a good book, trying to leash train her cats, or wishing she had a genie to do her bidding.

Ways to connect

https://www.sheilakellbooks.com

https://www.facebook.com/sheilakellbooks

https://www.goodreads.com/sheilakellbooks

https://www.bookbub.com/authors/sheila-kell

Sheila loves to hear directly from readers. Feel free to email her at sheila@sheilakell.com.

Don't miss out on new releases, exclusive excerpts, and giveaways! Join her newsletter: https://www.SheilaKell.com/subscribe

Join her Facebook Reader Group:
https://www.facebook.com/groups/sheilakellbooks